LIVES AND EMBERS
Jacob G. Rosenberg

JACOB G. ROSENBERG was born in Lodz, Poland, the youngest member of a working-class family. After the Germans occupied Poland he was confined, with his parents, his two sisters and their little girls, to the Lodz Ghetto, from which they were eventually transported to Auschwitz. Except for one sister (who committed suicide a few days later) all the members of his family were gassed on the day of their arrival. He remained in Auschwitz for about two months, then spent the rest of the war in other concentration camps. In 1948 he emigrated to Australia with his wife Esther; their only child, Marcia, was born in Melbourne. Rosenberg's poems and stories have appeared both in Australia and overseas. He has published three books of poetry in English, as well as three earlier volumes of prose and poetry in Yiddish. This is his first book of prose in English.

ALSO BY JACOB G. ROSENBERG

Poetry and prose in Yiddish

Snow in Spring
Wooden Clogs Shod with Snow
Light – Shadow – Light

Poetry in English

My Father's Silence
Twilight Whisper
Elegy on Ghetto (video)
Behind the Moon

Lives and Embers

Jacob G. Rosenberg

THE UNIVERSITY OF ALABAMA PRESS
Tuscaloosa

Copyright © 2005
Jacob G. Rosenberg

Published 2007 by The University of Alabama Press
Tuscaloosa, Alabama 35487-0380

First published in Australia by Brandl & Schlesinger, Book Publishers.

∞
The paper on which this book is printed meets the minimum requirements of
American National Standard for Information Science—Permanence of Paper
for Printed Library Materials, ANSI Z39.48-1984.

Rosenberg, Jacob G., 1922-
Lives and embers
"Fire Ant books"

ISBN-13 978-0-8173-5447-3 (pbk. : alk. paper)
ISBN-10 0-8173-5447-6 (pbk. : alk. paper)

Cataloging-in-publication data available from the Library of Congress.

In memory of my teachers

CONTENTS

LIVES

EMBERS

ACKNOWLEDGMENTS

A number of the stories in this collection have previously appeared in *The Australian Jewish News*, *Overland*, *Island*, *Meanjin* and *Eureka Street*.

I wish to express my gratitude to my editor, Alex Skovron, without whom this book would not have come to fruition. My appreciation also to Professor Louis Waller for his indispensable comments on the *Embers*; to Dr Mark Verstandig for his knowledgeable guidance with research; and to Professor Chris Wallace-Crabbe, who cordially agreed to read the manuscript and offered invaluable advice. Finally, I want to thank my wife Esther for her unfounded yet unequivocal belief in me.

'The truth of fiction is more profound, more charged with meaning than everyday reality.'

– *Eugène Ionesco*

PREFACE

In my fiction I tend to look upon life as a cosmic stage where illusions are the only reality we know. It is through these illusions, I believe, that we can sometimes better recognise our world, our fellow human beings, and even ourselves. Such is my hope for the short stories that I have gathered here under the rubric *Lives*. As for the *Embers* that comprise the second portion of the book, my inspiration for these miniatures has come from the method of biblical and Talmudic interpretation known as Midrash. Like poetry, the midrashic style – drawing upon scripture, legends and parables from antiquity to the present era – is not only terse in language but always ahead of its time. To me, it carries a universal liberating spirit, opening windows on the eternal ongoing human debate. Accordingly (and at the risk of trespassing on what is usually the province of the sages), some of the Embers in this collection are based on biblical and scriptural stories; others derive form old Yiddish folktales and wise utterances by simple people whom I had the good fortune to encounter and befriend on the difficult road of my enforced travels.

J.G.R.

LIVES

THE LADY IN THE POLKADOT DRESS

I have no evidence to prove the veracity of my story. I have no keepsakes, no tokens, even my pocket diary, in which I pencilled a few scanty notes, is gone. What's left is a memory. The memory of the intoxicating scent of lilac blossom at dawn. The miracle of sunrise, awakening the day from its nightly slumber. The hazy morning in mid-spring. But more than anything else, I remember the effervescent street where, among a young crowd full of laughter and vitality, I noticed the sad lady. She wore a white silk dress with black polkadots, and on her matching hat, like the wings of an exquisite blue butterfly, there trembled a translucent chiffon cockade. It seemed to me that she was gliding, hardly touching the ground, as if engrossed in an unearthly dance. I don't know why, but I was overcome by an almost insane compulsion to look into her alabaster, perhaps celestial face.

It was uncanny, like being caught up in some arcane tragicomedy. Why and how, I may never know; but I felt a powerful certainty that, although the woman had never met me, she knew, by means of some telepathic understanding, of my burning desire and was therefore deliberately ignoring me! My offended ego caught fire, and the pursuit took on a loathsome temper. I became impossibly aggressive. I grabbed at the hands of strange women as they passed by, earning screams and censorious glances, while all the time aware of a distant ironic smile on the lips of my unattainable lady. But to end this pursuit, this cat-and-mouse game, was now beyond my power: fate seemed to have taken control. I immersed myself in the depth of the crowd, thinking I would be swallowed up, as if in the waters of a black river, and somehow would surface to find myself face to face with her.

Suddenly I noticed that my passion had led me into a dilapidated tunnel-like gateway. A shrivelled gentleman with an ascetic expression stood there, in patent-leather dancing shoes, ankle-long black cape and top-hat; a hot-pink printed scarf hung around his neck, giving him the appearance of a circus clown. He stood silent and frozen as a monument – except for his tiny hands, which darted at a dazzling velocity as they juggled three shiny red clubs.

I was not more than a few steps away; a cloud of her delicious perfume lingered here. The sombre face of the ascetic clown was at rest. But his eyes, two black daggers, glittered with murderous contempt from under the brim of his stiff hat.

As if about to settle some score, I stormed off down the street. I felt an inexplicable anger with myself. Like a madman in a fury I pushed open the blue door of a dimly-lit coffee-shop and slammed my body into a chair at the nearest table, which was covered with a white, well-starched linen tablecloth. Out of thin air a tall, slightly stooped waiter appeared. I noticed that he had a nervous twitch in his left eye, and the Adam's apple in his scraggy throat jumped up and down violently. But his pallid face, beneath a pitch-black forelock, shone with an indescribable intellect and a profound wisdom.

Without asking me what I wished to order, he held out in his long bony fingers a glass of brownish-red cognac, and, pushing this almost under my nose, bent over me quite familiarly and flushed a little, as if about to reveal a forbidden secret. 'You are awaited in the national gallery. Please hurry.' He said no more.

The bill was tendered by a second character, corpulent with a bald head, who danced around me on his short bandy legs. He was eyeing me portentously, as if to say, *What's wrong with you, friend? Don't you recognise the man who just served you?*

The national gallery was packed with people, young and old, black and white. What a polyglot rhapsody rang through the air. They all had such happy open faces, as if caught up in a once-in-a-lifetime carnival, yet each with some personal reason to celebrate. It seemed to me that I alone was burdened of soul.

Dragging my feet as along a bottomless maze, I moved forward, jealously observing lovers walking arm in arm. All at once I became aware of the scent of that exquisite perfume I had encountered in the ancient gateway. Like a Rembrandt sunbeam, it lightened my melancholy disposition. As if by some gentle invisible hand I was drawn towards the source of my obsession. And when I came to a stop – oh my God! There, within the borders of a richly gilded frame, on a dark-green background akin to a luscious lawn in spring, in the shade of a blossoming lilac tree, there sat the woman of my dreams. I could almost hear her femininity singing from beneath her sleeveless polkadot dress. The tenuous rays of gallery light were reflecting longingly on her naked arms. She smiled at me – what a loving, lingering smile fluttered across her lips.

'It's not real, it's not real!' I cried out, and as the world staggered I seemed to be held aloft by the surprisingly strong arms of my black-forelocked waiter. His deep sonorous voice poured its warmth into my ear. 'Yes, art is fiction,' he said, 'but a fiction of the profoundest truth, such as no reality can ever hope to match. The woman you are pursuing lived a hundred years ago. It is the fiction of art that has ensconced her in the pantheon of immortality. The pantheon which, since time immemorial, has been the eternal refuge for our ephemeral existence. Only a blockhead insists that art is imitation of reality, of life. The reverse is true. Life draws from art, from poetry. Do you know how many revolutions have had their roots in romantic novels? How many freedom fighters learnt from such novels how to die, how to laugh into the hangman's face, crying out *Liberty!* at the very moment the noose silenced their voice?'

I tried to draw away, but he held me spellbound in his gaze.

'Look, over there,' he continued with even greater urgency. 'See that painting of starved little children being whipped by a pack of over-nourished bullies? Reality loves to forget, but art will remember. Mankind has refused to take art's warning seriously. Raskolnikov's justification of a murder evolved into the ideology of a whole nation. Perhaps of the whole world!'

'Yes, I know, I know.' I tried to catch my breath.

'To know is not enough,' he snapped. 'Many fools know, yet understand nothing. Knowing and understanding are very different things. At times they can be mortal enemies.'

As he threw his words into my face, his own was aflame. He must be a vision, I thought, a vision on fire. And even as my mind formed the notion, he began to recede, like a vision, into nothingness. But his deep sonorous voice, his fiery words, kept reverberating in my head like a great storm trapped in an ancient vessel.

Outside it had grown dark. Although there were no windows in the gallery, I could acutely sense the evening dimness, which had penetrated the stone walls and was filling the now-empty hall with the gloom of a humid fog. Slowly and with great care I began to move towards the door. But all at once I heard footsteps behind me – ever so feeble, and thin, like the footfall of a shadow at dusk. A burning desire to turn back took hold of me. But I was distracted by a sudden movement at the edge of my vision. It was an Orpheus, on a painting nearby – he appeared to be shaking his head! 'Don't,' he said sternly, 'or you will suffer my defeat.' I hesitated, but in the end I understood. I managed to reach the exit without turning – and felt a surge of joy as her moist hand folded into mine.

Beneath a sky dotted with promises we stood as if in a trance of ecstasy. As the young moon sailed timorously from cloud to cloud, I heard her melodious voice at last. 'I only have a minute,' she whispered. 'I cannot be away too long from my canvas, nor you from your mart of dreams. Look, the east is already turning grey. We must hurry.'

As she spoke, a slit of vivid blue opened up along the dark horizon. Time seemed to stop. Tenderly she disengaged her hand, and was gone. I looked down. There, in my own hand, I found a small bouquet of freshly picked forget-me-nots.

THE FATHER

In the early summer of his life, when he was still susceptible to unreasonable dreams and an inexplicit loneliness, Jon – poet at heart and a gifted painter – loved to leave for work well before the prescribed time. He would wander through the still-sleeping city, listening to the gentle sway of highrise buildings, to the chatter of stones, their nostalgic whispers of their life in the cosmos, before man had imprisoned them in the numb, cold, impersonal walls of the century's functional ziggurats.

Jon was a man of forty, a bachelor who held a senior position in the department of demography. He was tall, broad-shouldered, with a decent sense of humour. His pale complexion and dark storytelling eyes combined to radiate a naive sagacity. His professionalism in the department was exemplary.

Apart from his own duties, Jon also directly supervised the work of three clerical staff. There was young Peter, twenty-one, easy-going and open-faced, and irresistible to women – especially those older than himself, who wouldn't leave him alone. On top of that, Peter was an incurable gambler who claimed he made thousands on the races yet remained a hopeless pauper. No Friday ever went by without Peter leaving a 'hot tip' on Jon's desk. And although he knew that Jon was not a betting man and would not heed his advice, come Monday morning a downcast Peter would appear before his boss, humbly apologising for the 'bum steer', promising a hundred percent certainty next time.

Then there was Dorothy, a plumpish black-eyed brunette with a mole on her upper lip. She was in her mid-thirties, unmarried, highly strung, with the gait of an aggressive peacock. She was forever tightening the straps of her bra, sending her prominent bosom out ahead of her, on a mission perhaps possible...

And finally, Natalia. From the first day of her employment, Dorothy had viewed the thirty-year-old ginger-haired clerk with intense suspicion. She could not stand the way Natalia – her steel-rimmed glasses perched on her small upturned nose – took advantage of every free moment for reading; could not abide her constant cryptic doodling on scraps of paper; and above all could not forgive her strange faraway look.

But Natalia – lovely Natalia, with her innocent freckled face, a young European woman without a family – lived in a world of her own. A world, it seemed, of quixotic yet tangible realities, of impossible possibilities, where unreachable, outlandish desires are forever at hand.

While conscientiously absorbed in her duties, Natalia constantly sensed the presence of her amicable boss. She was impressed by his debonair fairness, his gentle approach to people, and she did everything possible to attract his attention. Intuitively she understood that although Jon was of the local landscape and climate, foreign to those she had known, there was something they had strongly in common – that inexplicable human hankering which does not recognise borders, a longing that can wipe away difference.

And so it was that one evening in winter, as Jon sat behind his desk sifting through the backlog of his duties, he found himself curiously aroused by an ingenious drawing of Dorothy made by Natalia, which had, it seemed, become lodged among the pages of a report she had brought him that day.

He knew that Natalia was not overly fond of the ever-suspicious Dorothy; yet the sketch revealed not only a certain compassion towards her co-worker, but something of her subject's inner mood, her hidden impulses and desires. When Natalia turned up for work the following morning, Jon greeted her with an inquisitive smile. She took it as her long-awaited cue.

On the stroke of six, well after their colleagues had gone for the day, Natalia knocked on Jon's door and entered his office, her briefcase under her arm. Without uttering a word she produced a watercolour drawing from the bag. It showed Jon sitting at his desk with a tie around his neck, but otherwise completely naked.

Jon was astounded, and embarrassed. What was the meaning of this? Yet he had to admit that the work was good, really good. He grinned at Natalia quizzically, trying to hide his unease. 'You're quite an artist,' he said.

'Well, I'd like to hope so,' the young woman replied, blushing. 'Though I don't necessarily paint things as they are,' she added hastily, 'but the way I see them, or the way they ought to be.'

'So, this...?'

'Your nakedness in this case is your exposure to the nature of the hypocritical system we serve. You see, where I come from, art without irony, or humour, or sometimes sarcasm, is no art at all.'

'Where exactly *do* you come from, Natalia?'

She was startled by the directness of the question, and hesitated. Then she seated herself in the visitors' chair, lit a cigarette and took a deep puff.

'Since you were speaking so eloquently,' Jon persisted, 'I'm really interested to know something about your background and what brought you to our shores.'

Natalia hesitated again, but only for a moment. 'Well, I was born in the lands of eternal winter,' she began, 'where snow covers your house for nine months of the year. I grew up among people with stony hearts and flashing fists, where the destiny of a young girl is decided by cruel men – father, brother, uncle, cousin. Do you want me to go on?'

'Please.'

'Our crippled neighbour, a middle-aged peasant called Stefan, made a deal with my father: a piece of Stefan's land for my younger sister, who was fourteen. Mother begged him not to do it, but he wouldn't listen. "Stefan is old and sickly," father argued, "in ten years he'll be dead. But meanwhile he'll give our lucky daughter many boys, and she'll make us rich." '

'Was it legal?' Jon cut in. 'Just fourteen...'

'Legal or not, it was quite customary. Anyway, the marriage never took place. The night before the wedding, the spirits that inhabit the bottom of all dark rivers invited my little sister to join them for supper...'

Jon could only shake his head in horror.

'You see,' Natalia went on, 'I was sixteen and next in line. Again my mother wept and begged her husband on her knees, but he was not to be moved. He was determined that this time his plans would bear fruit.

'Next morning, at the first spark of light, mother woke me and handed me a small basket with meagre provisions. "Go, my child," she told me. "And may God be with you." I walked for days, through knee-deep snowfields, knocking on doors and asking for shelter, for a piece of bread. There were some houses inhabited by good people, but the good ones, as a rule, have little to give. Until one day, perhaps the luckiest in my life, I arrived in a town where, after many enquiries, I found work.

'My employers were a young married couple, very much in love, who needed domestic help. Both were renowned painters. I worked hard, did everything to please them – they were such genuine people, I grew to love them dearly, and in time they treated me like a member of the family. I spent almost eight years there, they were the best years of my life. They opened up a new world for me with their art – they took an active interest in my natural ability to draw, and in the evenings they showed me how to develop my talent. *Art is not the mirror of life*, they would say, *but the other way round. The first stroke on a canvas is the painter's first step to inner freedom.'*

Jon was much taken with this young woman, her untamed demeanour, her uninhibited way of talking about her life. He couldn't help measuring her against the people around him – her honesty against their obliqueness, her self-exposure against their empty masks and hollow words. Yes, she appealed to him greatly, and although he had loved several times in his forty years, Jon knew that Natalia was different – very different indeed.

He invited her to his charming old bungalow, its walls over-grown with ivy and surrounded by native shrubs, in the city's south-eastern suburbs. He introduced her to his mother Andrea, no longer young but still spritely and attractive. He showed Natalia his own paintings and listened to her comments, they discussed art and many other things. He began to see her regularly outside of work. On Sundays they would explore the city's many galleries together.

Before long they had become intimate, and although they did their best to keep the relationship a secret, Dorothy – who had always hoped Jon might discover *her* – was the first to sense that something was afoot. Meanwhile, Peter – the ever-accomplished Don Juan – kept a quiet but eager watch on Natalia from the corner of his eye, marvelling at the woman's fidelity.

One evening after dinner, while Andrea allowed her long fingers to muse over the keyboard to the tune of a Chopin ballade, Jon invited Natalia into his studio, where a portrait stood on the easel. 'It's your late father, isn't it?' she said quietly.

'How can you tell?' he asked.

'Children always glorify their dead parents.'

'It's true. But Dad really was a great man, and a great father. Care for a glass of port?'

'That would be nice. Though perhaps we should ask Andrea to join us.'

As the three of them clinked glasses, Jon pointed to the portrait. 'It's not quite finished yet.'

'I can see that,' said Natalia. 'But the character of the man, and your love for him, already shine through.'

Jon smiled. 'When an artist paints a person, especially a person very dear to him, he must be guided primarily by love. Of course,' he hastened to add, 'this applies to any subject one wishes to immortalise on canvas.'

'In that case, what is the ultimate aim of art – to express love, or to show the truth?'

'Both.'

'Yes, Jon, that should be so. Yet when it comes too close to home, love has a tendency to overtake truth. That's why all self-portraits, even those by the great masters, should be viewed with a grain of salt. As my mentors used to say, *No human being, no matter how noble, is free of a touch of narcissism.*'

Andrea was inclined to agree, but refrained from commenting. She was listening with a great deal of pleasure to the voice of the young woman she hoped might become her daughter-in-law.

It was on a Monday morning some weeks later that Natalia failed to turn up for work. Since she had never missed a day before, Jon was slightly concerned, though by no means alarmed. No doubt she had slept in, or had a cold, and would phone the office shortly. But she didn't, and when she was absent on the Tuesday as well, Jon grew uneasy. He dialled her number once, twice, three times – there was no answer. The moment his work day ended he ran over to her rented apartment and pressed the bell. No response. Seriously worried now, he decided to wait. Beyond the staircase window, night was falling like a bad omen. Suddenly he heard steps coming up the stairs. It was an elderly man, obviously Natalia's neighbour, for he began fumbling for his keys right outside the door along from hers. 'Can you tell me,' Jon blurted out, 'if something has happened to the young lady who lives in the adjoining apartment?'

The man looked up. 'I saw her this morning.' But then he added: 'She came back again a few hours ago, packed up her things, and left.'

Jon did not know what to make of this. He was devastated. The moment he returned home, Andrea sensed that something terrible had befallen him, but her son wouldn't speak about it. He refused dinner and went straight to bed.

Next day, at mid-morning, Jon's phone rang in his office. It was Natalia.

He was overcome with relief, but a relief tinged with terror. 'What happened, Natalia? Why the secretive departure? What have I done to upset you?'

'Jon, please listen to me.' She sounded tense, but strangely calm. 'Jon, you're a fine man, a very fine man. And you deserve a better woman than I can ever be.'

'That's surely for me to decide! – Natalia, where are you? Can we talk about it?'

'No, Jon, I need time.' And with these words she hung up.

Over the days and weeks that followed, Jon changed – he was no longer the same person, but someone grown suddenly bitter and resentful. That happy-go-lucky Casanova, Peter, was the first to resign. Dorothy, who had dreamt that her boss would one day relieve her of her chastity, soon followed suit. Jon, disgusted with himself, was now practically alone at work.

One evening months later, as he was making his way down the winding staircase after locking up his office for the night, Jon spotted a hunched figure sitting on the top step of the first-floor landing. He approached cautiously, and as he looked into the half-shrouded face he let out a shout. It was Natalia!

'Jon…' She was dressed in rags and looked like a beggar – and she was very clearly pregnant! 'Jon,' she murmured, 'I have no one, and nowhere to go, please help me. I was a fool, I made a huge mistake.'

He was overcome by compassion, and a wild joy. 'Natalia, we all make mistakes,' he said. 'We all do.'

She held up her hand. 'I'm about to give birth,' she said. 'Please. Help me to a hospital.'

He drove her through the city streets at breakneck speed. There was no time for questions in Emergency, and fifteen minutes later a tiny baby girl was born. Natalia lay there, exhausted and pale as snow. In a voice almost inaudible she begged Jon's forgiveness. 'I understand, Natalia, I do under-stand,' he kept repeating. 'Please don't speak now. You must rest.' He bent down and placed his lips against hers. She closed her eyes.

She never opened them again.

Doctors rushed in, expressed their regret and their condo-lences to the father, told him his new daughter was fine. Later they asked him if he had decided on a name for the baby. Yes, he said. The little girl would be called Natalia.

Jon resigned from his position. Over the years that followed, with Andrea's help, he brought up the child. Little Talia blossomed, and was full of questions about her mother – whom Jon would describe as a princess born in a faraway place, a land of snow-white fables. 'That's why, in all these paintings that hang on your walls,' he told the child, 'the red cherries, green apples, black berries, all the purple and yellow roses – they always lie on an endless white bed of snow.'

On a sunny day in spring, just after eight-year-old Talia had returned from her day at school, a youngish man with a confident spring in his walk pushed open the wrought-iron front gate and began to negotiate the stony moss-covered path that led to the entrance of the now seldom visited house. Jon, who had been sitting on the veranda reading a book, rose from his cane chair and sauntered down the path. As soon as he recognised the uninvited guest, a smile broke across Jon's face. 'Peter, is it really you?' he shouted.

'Of course it's me,' cried the other. 'I was in the neighbourhood and thought I'd surprise my old boss. Mind you, it wasn't so easy to track you down.'

'Come in, Peter, come in and sit down… You must stay for dinner.'

'Thanks, but sorry, I can't. In two hours I'm due to fly out. I'm off to the States. First class – I have a new friend…'

Jon laughed. 'Still the same old Peter.'

'Why not? Life's too short.'

Drawn by the voices, Andrea and Natalia came out to investigate. 'This is an old colleague of mine. Peter, meet my mother Andrea, and my daughter Talia.'

A mischievous grin played across Peter's face. 'Jon, I didn't know you'd married.'

Jon looked down at his feet. 'My wife died in childbirth,' he said.

Peter paused, gazed for a long moment at Jon. 'Oh,' he said. 'I'm sorry.'

'Will you stay and have some tea with us?' Andrea asked.

'. . . Thank you, I'd love to, but unfortunately I'm pressed for time. I really only just stopped by to say hello. It's been far too long.' He held out his hand to Jon, bowed to Andrea. Then he turned to the freckle-faced Talia. 'May I kiss you goodbye, young lady?'

The little girl blushed. 'Only my father is allowed to kiss me,' she replied.

Peter smiled, bowed to the three of them, and walked slowly down the overgrown path. At the gate he turned and waved. 'Goodbye, then, Talia,' he called out, closed the gate behind him, and was gone.

MORDECHAI THE INTELLECTUAL

Everyone talked about Mordechai's intelligence. Foremost among his admirers was his wife Shifra. She would declare that what her Mordechai possessed in one finger wasn't to be found in the whole of Einstein's head. 'It's obvious,' she would explain, 'because I seldom understand what he is saying.' If Mordechai was aroused by a discussion, he would become so sharp as to be positively dangerous. He'd then shoot down any adversary with a barrage of fancy words, raising his finger skyward and announcing, 'Remember, it's all a question of abstract proletarian consciousness. The dialectical aspects of the matter are...' And so on.

Mordechai was a ladies' finishing tailor by trade, and a good one, who had arrived in Lodz in the early 1930s. He had come from a small town somewhere, and, as was common with small-town folk, he was a know-it-all. He understood things more quickly, more fully, and with greater insight than anyone else anywhere. At workers' meetings, he asked convoluted questions, his interjections were weighty, while his own speeches were fiery. His enthusiasm inspired them all, and with such an armoury of wisdom, understanding and rapier wit, he quickly rose to prominence in the local needleworkers' union. In fact, he became a star. There was not a placard posted, not a banner waved, not a strike called without Mordechai being on hand. He was involved in everything. Without him, there would have been neither union nor Party, and the world itself would have stopped turning. It was no wonder that young women were drawn to him like bees to honey. Shifra suffered agonies of jealousy, but for the privilege of living with such a great man she bore her grievance in silence.

Then war broke out. In the needleworkers' union there was confusion. A meeting was called. There were expressions of alarm: the Ribbentrop–Molotov pact was a betrayal! What was happening? What was going on? The only person who did not lose his head was Mordechai, who, with the agility of a circus acrobat, leapt on to a table and addressed the gathering, crying, 'Comrades! Remember! It is all still a question of abstract proletarian consciousness!' He threw this like a grenade into the midst of the disturbed assembly. For the moment, the reference to dialectical aspects had disappeared.

In the three weeks that it took the Germans to enter Lodz, Mordechai moved to the Soviet-occupied part of Poland with his wife, who was then in the late stages of pregnancy. There, for the first time and with great rejoicing, he met with Soviet soldiers, Voroshilov's comrades of whom he had read so much in the numerous foreign-language books and pamphlets he had devoured.

With rekindled enthusiasm, he prepared himself to educate the backward Jewish masses in Soviet truths, but his best intentions foundered. His services were not particularly sought by the propaganda office, and, early one December morning, two uniformed men appeared at his door and set in motion a chain reaction that had Mordechai, his wife and their newly born daughter, Lenina, dispatched on an excursion to the more distant, somewhat cooler provinces of Stalin's paradise on earth.

On the train Shifra cried. Mordechai pranced about her as though one leg had become shorter than the other.

'Shifra,' he kept saying, 'you don't understand. You're no better than all those other bourgeois geese who don't know the meaning of revolution, or of sacrifice for the cause, or of building a brave new world. You don't have the faintest notion of what the dialectical process is all about. So stop crying, Shifra, I beg you. It's embarrassing in front of all these fellow passengers.'

Shortly after their arrival at the Siberian camp, Shifra became aware of the Kalmyk overseer's oriental gaze, which fell repeatedly on her ample bust. It was now Mordechai's turn, she reasoned, to put up in silence. But Mordechai was not one to be silent. One day he approached the overseer and said, 'Comrade governor, I come to you with a plea. It is not about my wife; nor has it to do with my own honour. Revolutions have no place for such bourgeois notions. The issue is more truly one of proletarian consciousness and socialist integrity allied to morality as taught by our beloved Ilyich Lenin, by Comrade Stalin and by that intrepid knight Budenny, whom I feel I have come to know so well through the reading of his works.'

On hearing Budenny's name, the Kalmyk's eyes ignited with a wolfish fire. Next morning Mordechai was on his way to the mines of Sakhalin, there further to salt his dreams of revolution.

In the spring of 1945 the war ended. The world was free. Free! At the very sound of the word, Mordechai felt reborn.

In Lodz, to which she had by now returned, Shifra waited impatiently for Mordechai. Beside her at their reunion was their daughter Lenina, who was holding the hand of a little boy. This child had Shifra's appearance, except for the dark narrow eyes. Shifra smiled as she presented the child to Mordechai, saying, 'He's called Herschel, after my grandfather.'

Mordechai promptly accepted Herschel. As a member of the Party and an internationalist, he was also the builder of a new world in which there was no room for bourgeois prejudice. Mordechai had no time for trivialities. What was more important was that Poland needed him, and, as if nothing had happened in the six years of the war, he made straight for the union offices, where he set about establishing a cooperative, became an official and subsequently its delegate. However, his efforts to please his superiors and be useful – above all, to be useful to the cause – ended one night with another knock on the door. Across the threshold stepped an old comrade called Tadeusz who, with good reason, had also come to be known as Thumper. With Mordechai he was hearty.

'My dear Abrasha!' he said expansively.

'My name is not Abrasha,' replied Mordechai curtly.

'Oh, what droll people you Jews are. You do so insist on continually changing your names. Listen, Abrasha, I'm here as the representative of the Polish people. Tomorrow, at ten precisely, I want you to be at my office. You have information that we need. Names, for instance. Names; we want names; lots of names. In the meantime, you need have no fears for yourself. I am posting a guard at your front door for protection. You're safe. You have nothing to worry about. You're in good hands.'

Mordechai did not appear at Tadeusz's office. Instead, at first light, he, together with Shifra, Lenina and little Herschel, left by a secret rear door, thereby also leaving Poland behind forever.

In time, they reached the shores of a fortunate new country. It was not long before Mordechai acquired a workshop. He made rapid progress and very quickly became a manufacturer, in the process amassing a sizeable fortune.

On his retirement, Wednesday became his favourite day – it was the day that Shifra would leave early in the morning to go about her activities. Lenina was married to a doctor who hailed from a fine Chinese family; Herschel lived on a kibbutz in Israel. Mordechai was free, entirely free, able without distraction to sit in his customary armchair, watch his favourite television show, *Bonanza*, and indulge himself in sweet tea and nuts from a small table by his side.

On one such Wednesday, however, at a most crucial moment when Hoss was getting involved in a brawl, the doorbell rang tersely.

'Confound it,' Mordechai cursed to himself. 'Just as I'm relaxing, some beggar or other has to come visiting.'

Peering through the spy-hole in the door, he saw, beaded with sweat, a man he had come to consider a *nudnik*. The man carried a pile of books in his arms. Adopting as well as he could his Shifra's voice, Mordechai rasped from his side of the door, 'My husband isn't home at the moment and I have no money.'

'Shifra, dear,' he heard from the other side, 'I haven't come about money. I've brought him the last volume in the series he wanted.'

'He's read it already. A year ago.'

'How could he? It's just been published.'

'Well, as far as I know he's read it,' insisted Mordechai, tiptoeing back to his place and to his favourite program.

But as he sank into his armchair, Mordechai's head slumped forward. He suddenly found himself in another world. He was in a grand red marble palace. On a gilded throne sat Karl Marx chewing on a large marrowbone. To his right, dressed in women's clothes, stood Stalin himself, drinking bile, and to his left, naked except for a nappy, stood Lenin – addressing him, Mordechai, in the warped metallic tones of a robot.

'Mordechai. You have sinned greatly. A terrible punishment awaits you. You have associated with Bundists, and Zionists, and Trotskyists. You have given money to Israel...'

'No! No! I have had no such associations,' stammered Mordechai in defence. 'I've merely wanted to persuade them, convert them, influence them, convince them of the truth. As for my contributions, they were just small change and, even then, solely on your behalf, sir. . . '

'And what is this?' boomed Stalin, and at that instant there appeared before Mordechai a huge television screen, on which he could see his son with the slanting Asiatic eyes standing to attention as Yitzhak Rabin pinned a medal of valour on his chest.

'So!' Stalin snorted, this time seeming to speak with the voice of the one-time Kalmyk overseer of the camp to which Mordechai had been sent. 'Kidnapping Soviet children is socialism too!'

Mordechai felt faint, confused. When he came to, he saw Shifra hovering over him, her whole demeanour stark and tormented, like that of a frightened bird.

'Mordechai dearest! Mordechai!' she appealed to him. 'What happened? What's the matter, dear? Tell me, Mordechai, what is it, what is it?'

Mordechai looked into he face, her eyes.

'Nothing has altered,' he murmured, 'nothing has changed. Nothing. It's all still a question of abstract proletarian consciousness, of abstract proletarian consciousness, while the dialectical aspects of the matter. . . '

And, even as he spoke, he turned to one side, pressed his head into the white cushion on his chair and, with the smile of all-knowingness on his lips, fell soundly asleep like a tired child.

EMBERS OF LIVES

When still a young man I was exiled from my place of birth and forced to travel from culture to culture, language to language, quite often from the astonishing to the bizarre. Somehow I always managed to find shelter within myself, especially when no shelter was to be found elsewhere. I would discover, at such times, a persistent need to relive those precious days when I had been safe and happy by the hearth in my parents' house.

I could see my self-taught father, the eternal doubting optimist, two silver-grey eagle eyes beneath his tightly knit brows, eating up the words from his open book. I'd often wondered what would happen to the blank pages once all the letters had found their way into his stomach.

And mother, in a pale-blue linen dress with gilded buttons, sitting beside a vase of fragrant lilac, serene in the shadow of our swooning lamp, darning and mending as she hummed her daunting life:

My sun sinks into twilight,
Who will my light redeem?
My years the winds took care of,
My youth a childhood dream.

I could see myself there too, gazing into the slightly ajar window. The golden moon, veiled in my mother's gauze curtains, reads my mind. For on the other side of the wall, my adored Inka is reclining on her bed, blowing soap balloons and musing of love.

Yes, we were in love, very much in love – she the mature buxom sixteen-year-old romantic poet, and I her foolish pimple-faced Paul.

My world has been destroyed and rebuilt anew many times, yet the years have not erased the memory of the green fire of Inka's slightly slanted eyes; of her hair, parted in the middle, that fell like a blond waterfall from her shapely head; of her smooth dark skin, her full and ever-anxious lips, her soothing voice.

Inka would tell me that her father, gentle by day, brutalised her mother in the darkness of night – that he mounted her over and over again; that her mama moaned, pleading for mercy, and yet never let go of him, never. How feverishly Inka's story ignited my imagination, how swiftly we would dart off into the twilight of our secretive attic, how madly we embraced, kissed, touched, as I clumsily unbuttoned her blouse to release those tender round breasts, which I would cup in my palms and suck at, while she kept repeating, 'Oh Paul, my Paul, what a fool you are.'

In the autumn of 1939 war broke out, and within seven days the town of my birth was in the hands of vandals. They quickly imposed a curfew, plunged the streets into darkness, and punished the slightest transgression with death. One midnight, while our sombre three-storey tenement dozed in its restless slumber, I heard an urgent knock on our door. It was Inka's father, our good neighbour of many years, dressed in black like an undertaker. He had come to say goodbye. 'We're leaving town,' he said curtly, shaking my father's hand. His wife cried as she kissed my mother. My Inka, pale as a ghost, beckoned me aside and whispered into my ear, 'Paul, I'll be back soon.'

Well, it wasn't soon; it wasn't soon at all.

Thirty years later, in the land I now call home, I was browsing in a city bookstore one drizzly afternoon when I heard a voice – a strangely familiar, sweet, soothing voice from a never-forgotten past. 'Would you happen to have a copy of Celan's poetry in stock?' it said. I looked over towards that voice, and as she turned her head in my direction I saw the green fire in the slightly slanted eyes and I cried out: 'Inka, oh, Inka! Is it really you?'

'Yes, Paul, it's me,' she responded after a moment, in a rather dismal tone. Very much so.' I was taken aback. Did she not know how deeply she was still engraved upon my heart?

'Inka, please, we have to talk,' I blurted out. 'There is so much I want to know – *have* to know.'

'Yes, there is,' she replied with a weary sigh.

The salesgirl had returned. 'Sorry,' she said, 'we don't have any poetry by Celan.'

'Never mind,' I jumped in. 'I have a wonderful edition – I'll be happy to lend it to you.'

The next day, book in hand, I crossed the threshold of her neatly decorated apartment. The walls of the living room were constructed of books. Near a heavily curtained window stood a small grand piano. There was a mahogany table set off to one side, supported by six chairs upholstered in burgundy-coloured velvet. Inka stood in the centre of the room, a stoic heroine out of a Gogol story. Her dress was black, her blouse equally black and buttoned to the neck, but trimmed with white silk lace.

'So, Paul,' she said calmly, breaking the silence. 'After all those years, all those tragic events, you still remember me.'

'*Remember* you?' I cried. 'How could I ever forget you?'

'How?' she smiled sadly. 'We'll soon come to that.'

My head was bursting with the things I wanted to say. 'Please, Inka,' I managed. 'Tell me what happened to you and your family after we parted.'

'Well, I'm sure you know the story,' she said. 'Ultimately we all shared a similar fate, so we can skip the details of that chapter. When the war ended I began to look for you. Only for you. There was nobody else, my parents were murdered the day we arrived at the camp, and as you know I had no siblings. So you were the only link to my past, my only hope.

'There is not a land, not a city, where I didn't search for you, but no one knew, no one had heard about you. Until one day – not long after I arrived here, just two years ago – I was spotted by one of your friends, and before I had opened my mouth he blabbered out: "Inka, your Paul is here. He came after the war, with a wife and child." Obviously, lover, you were in a great hurry.'

Her words stung me. 'Please, Inka, please. We have had enough bitterness in our lives.'

'Well, you wanted to know, and I'm only telling you what is true. Why didn't you try to contact me? Why? And now here I am, a widow with two divorced daughters and five grandchildren, and you are a married man.'

'So what?' I retorted vehemently. 'Isn't there such a thing as friendship?'

'Of course there is. But friendship – with a man who is familiar with the birthmark between one's thighs – can make for a very complicated amicability. How do you think I would feel, Paul, sitting at the table with your wife and playing the game of innocence?'

'But what about *us*?' I shouted, though my confidence was tarnished by a pang of doubt.

'Us?' Inka repeated. 'You can't be serious.'

'I am. I know we're still in love.'

She let her hands drop in exasperation. 'Paul, what men cannot grasp is that a ten-year-old girl is already a little mother, while an old married man is still a boy. And that's not all.' She paused, shook her head. 'A woman can only live in one world at a time, whereas a man can live in two worlds, or more. I beg you, Paul, for the sake of both of us, don't come here again.'

And yet I kept on coming, week after week, month after month, until one evening, after I had entered her apartment clutching a bouquet of fresh red roses, Inka latched the door behind us and stood there for a moment, a mysterious smile – half tender, half resigned – lingering on her lips...

Afterwards she said to me: 'I can still recall so vividly, Paul, that night all those years ago, when your parents went to a wedding and left us alone in the house. How strong and impatient you were, how you swore eternal devotion, how sweetly we merged. I have never ever loved a man more than I loved you then.'

'And now, Inka? What about now?'

'Yes, I still love you – otherwise we wouldn't be here like this. But love, real love, is not just a creaking bed. It's so much more. And above all, it's the awareness of what is hurting your lover. Paul, this was what you wanted. I suppose I wanted it too. Just this once. But to continue now would only create more pain, more anguish. For you and for me. So please – you must promise me you'll never come back here again.'

For several weeks I endured a tormented existence, and could think of nothing but Inka. I wrestled with myself, trying desperately to respect her wish, arguing with myself whether this was really what she wanted. I drove past her building countless times, I looked up at her window; but those heavy curtains remained forever drawn.

Then, one sombre autumn afternoon, my resolve failed and I found myself mounting the staircase to Inka's apartment again. As soon as I reached her landing I noticed a white envelope, marked *Paul*, taped to the door-handle. With quivering fingers I unsealed it and withdrew a folded piece of paper. It contained a short poem:

From the heavy darkness behind us
There can not be another May;
Soap balloons shine, then vanish
In spring on a windy day.

I spent that night in the local park, on a bench beneath a flickering lantern. I sat there, breathing the moist scented air of the park, resigned to my irretrievable loss, pondering the serendipities of life. Loneliness is much lonelier at night. As I reread Inka's poem for the hundredth time, my miscarried youth rose up before me – rose up like a soap balloon, twisting and spinning and all the while hovering out of reach, into the springs of windy days.

CONFESSIONS OF A CLOWN

My name is Ilya, when I was a little boy they called me Ilyoshka. I was seven when we left Moscow and came to Paris. It was just after the Bolshevik Revolution. We moved into a luxury apartment, in one of the most prestigious quarters of the city. My father, Raymond, was clever in business; he had made his money in furs, travelling between Moscow and the German city of Leipzig. Papa was a burly man with a heart of gold, a typical Russian. He drank lots of vodka, but not once did I ever see my father drunk. Papa also liked to sing, his baritone voice was well suited to the sadness of Russian song. 'Papa, why are these songs so sad?' I once asked him. 'You see, Ilyoshka, the Russian song is a tale of the people's endless suffering.' 'But why, Papa, why do they suffer so much?' 'A good question, son, a good question,' and he left it at that. I loved my father. Unfortunately he was seldom at home.

Neither was Mama, though for different reasons. My mother, Viola, was in her late thirties at the time. She was a tall blonde with a dark complexion, and the feline glint in her green eyes could murder a man. A confirmed socialite with an army of lovers half her age, Mama was a compulsive liar. She was also a frightful cynic with a scorpion for a tongue, and her artistry at blaming others for her misdeeds was phenomenal. I am the sole heir, thank God, of all those wonderful qualities.

I was brought up by our housemaid Yolanda, a girl from a nearby village who liked to stay indoors. I was an only child. Sixty years later I can still recall Yolanda's strong hands and her alabaster-white breasts. She loved me to suck on the dark-red nipples, for which my special reward was always a glass of hot chocolate. I became so accustomed to this pleasure that the moment she brought me home from school I would ask, 'Yolanda, can I get a glass of hot chocolate?' 'Sweet little devil,' she would murmur, unbuttoning her cotton blouse.

There was one more ritual that must be mentioned in my confessions. Bathtime. This was something we both looked forward to. No sooner had the sun begun to set than Yolanda would grow restless and start running a bath. There was not an inch of my body that she neglected to soap. She continued with this practice long after I had reached puberty. Now, as a bachelor in my late sixties and a frequent guest at many international bordellos, I can state quite authoritatively that I have never met another woman whose skills could equal Yolanda's.

One day, I think it was a Sunday – yes, Yolanda's church day; after all, our housemaid was a religious zealot – Papa flew in unexpectedly from Moscow and there, at the kitchen table, sat Mama's latest lover, devouring his breakfast. Clever Mama jumped the gun. 'Raymond, darling,' she beamed. 'Am I glad to see you! Ten minutes more and you would have missed the chance to meet a distant cousin on my mother's side, Giacomo Francati. He was passing through Paris, and by a lucky coincidence managed to find me. He was just about to leave.' Papa nodded and walked off to his study.

That evening when I was already lying in my bed – and Yolanda, as usual, had left the door to my room ajar because, like Mama, I was afraid to sleep alone – I could hear Papa complaining about the disorder on his desk and some missing money; the name Giacomo Francati came up. Mother hit back, aggression was in her blood, she quickly turned the tables and blamed the whole situation on Papa's absence. My father, as ever, apologised. Then, as if to divert attention from a painful topic, he asked: 'What about Ilya? Do you ever check over his homework? Do you talk to his teachers?' 'Of course I do,' she lied. 'And you should see how well he gets on with Yolanda. I promise you, Raymond, Ilyoshka is brilliant. He will undoubtedly become a doctor – yes, nothing short of a doctor.' 'Viola, don't you think that one first has to become a *mensch*?' Mother flew off the handle. 'Over my dead body,' she cried. 'There's enough of those already, and not enough of the others!' Just who the others were I didn't know, but although my heart was with Papa I believed that Mama was right. The word *mensch* meant then, and to this day still means, nothing to me. To be sure, I blame my mother for that.

Blaming someone else for my own delinquency became a potent and profitable tool in my adult life. I was thrice engaged, and thrice broke up, and each time I made the poor girl's family pay, though it was I who had violated *my* promise. At the age of forty I lost both of my parents. Yolanda, whom I had secretly pledged to marry, I threw out of the house. Later I wept, yet I had accused her of corrupting me. Why? I'll never know. Something in me was rotten and evil, I knew that what I was doing was not right but I couldn't stop myself. Many times I called out to my dead father for help, begging him to instil in me his generosity, his decency. But he would not respond; Mama must have stood in his way.

Thanks to my teachers I had no proper education. Nevertheless, I was cunning and I was streetwise. Consumed by a desire for fame, I began to write; but without success. I was told that to be a writer one had to read, and I had no head for books. Then one day, quite unexpectedly, I found the solution: public speaking. Yes, I would become a public speaker, an orator. How did this come about? Very simply. I happened to walk in on a lecture in a local hall, it was about *The Science of Morality*. A bespectacled man dressed in black was standing on a platform at the front of the room. 'Yes, gentle people,' he declared. 'For the sake of the higher Truth, one does have the right to cheat and to lie!' *Lie?* I asked myself. *In that case, Ilyoshka, what are you waiting for, you're a natural!*

In no time at all I became the most sought-after voice in the community. I frequently spoke to groups and societies of very diverse beliefs. In the morning I might give a talk before a school of socialists, to whom I proclaimed Marx as *Humanity's Saviour*; that very afternoon I would address a reactionaries' club and denounce him as *Humanity's Bane*. To a union of non-believers I would thunder that *God Is Dead*; to an assembly of the religious I would extol *Our Ever-Living Lord*. Certain of my friends – or rather acquaintances, for I have no friends and am friend to none – pointed out the hypocrisy in my behaviour. What a miserable lot they were, green with envy!

However, in order not to run out of material I began to pay daily visits to bookshops – not to buy, which in my opinion is a waste of money, but, as it were, to plunder – that is, to compile lists of dozens of writers, titles and critics, and to copy down the intelligent comments that one finds on the backs of most books. I would rush home and doctor the quoted pronouncements so adroitly that their own authors could never have recognised them. These achievements gave me not only the legitimate right to claim my place among the *literati*, but the privilege to express a respected opinion about reading and writing, even about the choice of volumes that should be displayed on one's shelves.

On the back of one of the many books that passed through my hands, I read that a handsome well-dressed fool will socially outclimb any plain-looking sage. Well, along with Mama's art for lying, cheating and cynicism, I had also inherited her good looks, and my sartorial tastes were beyond reproach. Which meant that I was morally entitled to lead. Imbued with such grandiose notions, I was traversing a city square one morning and happened to look across at the statue of the heroic general that graced it. The old boy, ensconced in bronze, stood helpless as two pigeons alighted on his bald head and brazenly deposited their droppings there. I was outraged. A law would have to be passed to teach birds respect. Otherwise, how would *I* defend myself from such indignities when the day came for *my* likeness to be erected up there on that plinth?

A week before May Day, Paris was paralysed by a general strike: no taxis, no Métro, no mail, no daily papers – what an incredible prelude to my debut on the stage of world history! After all, was I not a child of the Bolshevik Revolution? A disturbing silence reigned over the city in the pre-dawn hours of the first of May. The only signs of life were a few eager citizens – with red carnations in their lapels, like me – crossing a road or running an errand, anxiously awaiting the unfolding of this decisive day.

I knew that I had to calm myself: the tension, the expectation was almost unbearable. When I mentioned the decisiveness of the day, just then, I was referring to my own position, my own place in the wider scheme of things, my hope of being catapulted to the very apex of social recognition. So you can imagine my joy when all at once, a few blocks away, at the far end of one of the city's great boulevards, I espied a mass of demonstrators marching into view, billowing like a mighty armada beneath a forest of red sails. Before I knew it, and as befitted a man of my standing, I had joined the front ranks of the jubilant multitude. Above me burned a silent sky of promise; behind me swirled a stormy sea of open mouths, hypnotically chanting 'Long live...! Long live...!'

Here I deftly injected the name *Ilya*. The sound of my name was infectious, it was quickly taken up by the crowd until the whole throng was singing: 'Ilya, Ilya! Long live Ilya!' Believe me, who-ever did not see me there, whoever did not remark upon my charisma shining forth from within that broil, has seen no beauty in his life.

The sea of people arrived and assembled in a large central square, where a platform was hastily erected. I invited myself to a prominent place on the podium. A pale middle-aged man was standing at the microphone. He had the face of an old goat but he came straight to the point. 'Comrades, fellow workers,' he shouted. 'We find ourselves in the midst of a monumental drama. You are all acquainted with the details of our great agenda. So, without any further ado, I give you – our Ilya!'

The silver microphone was in my hand, the massed choir took up its chant once again. 'Ilya, Ilya! Long live Ilya!' they sang. I cleared my throat. 'My dear beloved comrades,' I intoned. 'My fellow workers. Today marks a new beginning. Tomorrow belongs to us. Our oppressors are in disarray. They will oppress us no longer. Soon it will be our turn to pass judgment upon them. We will be the new masters, and they will know what it means to be a slave.' At these words the whole assembly burst into wild cheering. They shouted and clapped and stamped their feet. I knew I had them now, in the palm of my hand.

Then something totally unexpected happened: I stopped – and did not know what to say next! The harder I tried, the less I could recall of all those quotations I had copied out so assidu-ously from the backs of books. Floundering, I mouthed the names of a few obscure poets and philosophers who had nothing to do with my oration.

Suddenly it dawned on me what was happening. My poor father's disdain for the Bolsheviks flashed before my mind; I could feel his hatred towards Stalin, the cruel dictator who had made him flee the country of his birth; I could hear the disenchantment and the sadness in his voice. The voice seemed to open out within me, struggling to be released. The voice became *my* voice, and – before I knew it, there I was, unconsciously blurting out my Papa's deepest political sentiments, his bitterest anti-revolutionary invective!

A tremor ran through the crowd, a buzz, a gasp of amazement that rapidly turned into a collective explosion of wrath. Within seconds they had been transformed from an army of disciples into an ugly mob. There was a new kind of fire and fury in its eyes. I was surrounded, jostled, hurled to the ground. They were trampling me underfoot, kicking at me, swinging their fists into me. 'Traitor!' they screamed. 'Death to the traitor! Death to all traitors!' Over the din, through a fog of pain, I thought I could hear Mama's voice: *Ilyoshka, my darling son. This is your first reward for aspiring to be a mensch.*

As I crouched there, doubled over in agony and despair, her words from years ago grew stronger and echoed in my skull. *Remember, Ilyoshka, it is much better to deal with one noble pleb than with a pack of vulgar aristocrats. A lady who has turned prostitute is far preferable to a prostitute who plays the lady. The latter will never forgive you. . .*

Late that evening, in my darkened room, gazing into the image before me in the mirror, pondering my future, I let out a scream and, to my own bewilderment, threw both of my fists into the ebony shine of the looking-glass. The blackness shattered and I slumped to the floor beneath a shower of bleeding splinters.

Lying there in a pool of blood, listening to the shuffle of the advancing night, I kept scanning the story of my heart, wondering what had happened, asking how it could be. All of a sudden I saw Yolanda. Her face, partly obscured behind a black veil, was heavily made up; she was weeping. With fingers crippled by arthritis, she was trying desperately to unbutton her cotton blouse. *No more! No more!* I shouted, and fell back like a defeated clown – an absurd, grotesque creature crumpling into the centre of his circle of sawdust, outlined within a circular cage of blazing light, under the gaze of infinitely ascending circles of laughing, jeering, relentless humanity...

When at last I opened my eyes to the encompassing blackness, it was there, hovering above me. Mama's seductive feline smile.

GHETTO VECCHIO

I arrived at Venice on the first day of spring in the year 1599. It was long past the curfew, the streets lay numb, deserted. On a grey turret near the sleeping Rialto stood a huge cormorant. From time to time it opened its two black umbrella wings, as if preparing to attack. I wondered if it was the lingering smell from the fish mart, or perhaps its predatory instinct, which had brought it here.

The young gondolier, though I paid him well, was not happy to take me across the murky waters at such a late hour, and as we glided soundlessly past the Doge's palace, which overlooked the basin of San Marco, he crossed himself three times. It was almost one o'clock before I fronted the locked gates that isolated the children of Abraham, Isaac and Jacob from Christian Venice. A yawning guard charged with keeping the Jews locked up – at their own expense – gave me an inquisitive look. Hey, who the hell are you? What is it you want? Don't you know it's forbidden for your kind to loiter outside the Ghetto walls at this hour?

But sir, I have money.

Now you're talking – all you Hebrews do.

But sir, how did you know that I am what I am?

A guard knows. He has a dog's sense of smell. One of your kind may wear a Florentine cloak, with a big cross on his chest, and he may call himself His Highness, Alberto Benvenuto di

Fiore, yet a man like me will sniff out in an instant that, behind the richly embroidered mantle, his lordship with the golden crucifix across his bloated belly is really a Baruchi swine. By the way, what sort of money have you got – gold or paper?

Both, sir.

Of course, you would. I knew at once that I was dealing with a gentleman – and *dealing* is the right word, because I have an inborn aversion to bribers and blackmailers. So, where was I? Oh yes, I almost forgot. Just before your welcome appearance, young Guglielmo was here – you know, master Will.

Which Will?

Will – Will the bard.

The bard?

Yes. He always comes at night. Flies like the wind, in a black cloak and mask.

What for?

Apparently he is writing a play, or so they say. Though my professional experience tells me that his constant visits to Giudecca have some deeper, uncanny, perhaps even sinister meaning. Only God knows if among his ancestors there doesn't hover the skullcap and scorched beard of some cobwebbed Iberian rabbi.

What an intriguing story. But please, sir. Be a good man and open the gate. I am rather pressed for time.

Very well, I will. But don't you think that a man of my standing needs to be paid in advance for his labour?

How much?

The lot! Everything you have.

Everything?

Yes, my little prince. Let me relieve your pockets of their burden. You know the rules, don't you?

Sure I know. I experienced them in my bygone future.

It was dark. In Giudecca, lights were permitted only at certain prescribed hours. But a man like me has no trouble finding his way about a ghetto, even with eyes closed. And so, before long, I stood beside my father's dearest friend, Rabbi Judah Aryeh Modena.

Ah, I knew you'd be coming tonight.

How, rabbi? How did you know?

I have my ways of knowing. Or maybe, let us say, I had a wink from above. There are things one never knows how one knows. But what's new at home, Daniel? Is my friend, your father, still behind bars?

Yes, rabbi, he is. And they won't even let us see him, not even mother. We are told he has been tortured, kept for hours on the rack. They want him to confess, to give them the names of all the Marranos he has successfully brought back to our fold. They have promised that if he complies, they will grant the mercy of strangling him to death before they burn him at the stake.

Rabbi Judah dropped his head in silence. From the open *Gemara* he picked up his white handkerchief to stem the tears filling his red-rimmed eyes.

You know, Daniel, I lost my Hannah to childbirth, and while I was still in mourning someone denounced my brother Emanuel – for instilling hope in the hearts of our despairing brethren by heralding the coming of the Messiah. Emanuel was arrested and after a merciless beating, bleeding all over, he was brought to face the Inquisition. Is it true, Emanuel, asked the frowning inquisitor, that you have denied the presence of our Redeemer? Noble sir, he replied, do you not think that my bleeding head, my open wounds, my broken limbs, confirm his absence? Very good, Jew. We will soon discover how well your ebullient wit sustains you on your journey to Hell...

But our Almighty, whose name will shine forever, heard my brother's inner voice and, just an hour before the execution, He sent an angel to collect Emanuel's soul. The Inquisition refused to be cheated, however. They roped my brother's broken body to a pole and set it alight just the same. And then, according to bystanders, something very strange took place, something no one can account for. As the flames engulfed my brother, his corpse suddenly opened its blackening mouth and gave out a thunderous peal of mocking laughter. A deep shudder, like the Devil's whisper, ran through the crowd; crazed with fear, they took off in all directions.

Within hours a rumour had spread among our people, and among the gentiles too. Someone swore that, at midnight, at the site of the execution, he had seen a floating, translucent silhouette rekindle the ash into a living flame. And indeed, by daybreak it was confirmed that a fire was still burning there. The Inquisition, enraged, ordered the fire to be extinguished – but it refused to succumb, either to water or to sand. Only when one of the inquisitors suggested that they should make use of the fire to torch another ten Jews, did the flames revert swiftly to a pile of lifeless ash.

Rabbi Judah paused and took a deep breath.

Yes, it's now five years since God took my Hannah. And in all those years I haven't stepped outside these walls. So tell me, Daniel, how fares Venice beyond the Ghetto – Venice, with her sombre bridges and murky canals, her gilded Byzantine arches and mercantile pomposity? How fares this meretricious queen?

Nothing has changed, rabbi, nothing. Venice is all sugar-coated bitterness, swelling pockets, shrinking hearts, the joy of hollow laughter. Still the same motley world of betrayal and daily contrivance. The only novelty is the ferocious conflict between the privileged Levantine Jews and the New Christian community. You probably heard of that farcical recent trial. For upholding Venetian law, and for the sake of his flesh, a Jew had to pay with his soul. And still our Redeemer tarries ... tarries. Why, rabbi? Why? Is it perhaps because He is waiting for us to become worthy to receive Him? If that's the case, rabbi, He may never come.

You may be right, son, you may be right. And yet we are not released, even for one minute, from believing that our Anointed stands on our very threshold.

It was late dusk when I took my leave. A clammy vapour arose from the bleak canals of Venice, and high above my head the darkening sky came alive with thousands of shimmering questions and rustling sighs. My gondolier, a middle-aged man of few words, pointed at the unusually bright moon, indicating the danger of my transit. Nevertheless, as we glided along, the murmur of the water was soothing. In the back of my mind I pondered Rabbi Judah's wisdom. Men and Messiah, I reflected despondently. Like two banks of the same canal, they run parallel with one another, and yet remain so very, very far apart.

THE MERCHANT

No one knew when he was born, or whence he came. He was just there, a quiet, slightly melancholic man; a low-profile gentleman of great wealth and noble benevolence whose aversion to blood and cruelty was renowned. And yet, in the face of even the most barbaric of laws, he would proclaim, without the merest blink of an eye: *The law of the land is the law.*

He was always attired in a charcoal-grey cape, fastened at the neck with a primrose brooch. He wore black hose, narrow breeches, a dark-brown doublet with embroidered sleeves, and boots of the finest Iberian leather; on his head sat a soft Florentine cap which he seldom took off.

He was a shipper by trade, and a player on the stock exchange. But money was not what drove him. His aim, as he himself declared – though not without a sense of modesty, and perhaps also to ingratiate himself into the hearts of the ordinary folk, for whom wealth meant foreignness – his aim was to save people, especially those who had fallen into the hands of merciless usurers. And although no one ever actually witnessed him at his self-appointed trade, no one doubted the truth of his assertion, especially the judicial authorities of the time.

I met him at the inn of the Holy Angel, which stood half-awake by the edge of a sleepy lake. He was sitting alone and looked rather vexed; a rowdy group of the companions he constantly entertained had already departed. So had his beloved kinsman, a young but ever-bankrupt knight who had apparently just fallen madly in love with a rich and generous maiden.

To forestall any suspicion that I was a beggar looking for alms, I immediately introduced myself. 'I am Zachariah ben Isaac Halevi, sir. Born in Benghazi, eldest son of a wise and well-to-do cobbler.'

'*How* well, ben Isaac?' asked the merchant with a prosperous smile.

'Well enough, sir, to reward you handsomely if you can provide his son with a safe passage back home.'

'And how wise?' the merchant persisted, his eyes closing.

'My father, dear sir, can accurately judge the character and profession of any person by examining a worn-out pair of his shoes. He can tell if the wearer of the shoes was a marabout or a thief, a homebody or a vagabond, a damsel or a whore.

'That's really amazingly wise,' said the merchant, still with his eyes closed. 'What a wonderful man he must be, this Isaac the cobbler. Unfortunately I cannot tell you anything about my pro-genitors. I know as much about my past as any man knows about his future. Though in the back of my mind, somewhere in the foggiest regions of my reluctant memory, there rings an echo, too, of a cobbler's name – it tolls in my head like the dying chime of an ancient forsaken churchbell. A certain Simon the cobbler...'

The merchant drew a deep breath, as if shaking himself free of the echo. 'Would you care to have a glass of Rhenish?' he asked. 'And if you will, let me assure you, ben Halevi, that your passage home has been granted.'

'My thanks to you, sir. But pray tell me, great benefactor, why do you speak to me with your eyes closed? Am I so ungainly to look at?'

'Not at all, Zachariah, not at all,' he laughed. 'I do this quite inadvertently. And although I do not know how or from where this habit came to me, yet over the years I have grown convinced that with closed eyes I can better see my own thoughts, before they emerge into words. Take note, my young friend: we live in an age when a man – for his own benefit, and for that of his friends – must constantly probe the image of his thoughts before he sends them out on their journey.'

'Sir, you speak almost with my father's tongue. Before I departed he advised me to leave my language at home, *until the weather broke*.'

'Zachariah, the more I hear about your father, the more I like him. Obviously he and I have much in common.'

'Yes, master, that is true. For again, as my father would declare, *wisdom is a healing for one's heart*. He says that all wise people, no matter where they come from, will one day come to worship at the mountain of eternal truth. I also heard him say – and this may amuse you, sir – that when the Messiah arrives, all people will become sages, except the fools. Do you know why? Because they think they already are.'

The merchant smiled. 'Zachariah, is your father a God-fearing man? And to which God does he bow? Does he pray to the east, or does he, like many other people of the south, worship the gods of darkness?'

At this moment the conversation was abruptly cut short. A young knight flew in, and hastily kissed the merchant on the brow. The merchant whispered something to the youth – some kind of promise, something about three thousand ducats. 'May my beloved kinsman be fortunate in his amorous endeavours,' he added wistfully, as the young man darted off into the night.

Meanwhile the inn was coming to life again: with husky, swarthy, shirtless oarsmen, their necks adorned with red kerchiefs, and crudely-painted professional ladies – though none of the latter dared offer their services to the merchant. They all knew he was bound to his knightly young kinsman.

'The shipper trusts his ships, but the winds laugh,' murmured the merchant. 'I fear I shall be handsomely rewarded with cudgels.'

Suddenly overcome by a great affection for this mysterious man, I stood up and placed my hand on his shoulder.

He smiled and nodded. 'I hold the world but as the world, Zachariah. A stage where each of us must play his part. Mine, I'm afraid, is a sad one.'

THE USURER

In the land of famous waterways, crafty merchants and great art, there lived a man, a professional usurer, known as Ezra. He inhabited a solid cottage with a black-tiled roof which stood at the end of the street, apart from every other house. Ezra's attire, his gait and, notably, his habits were greatly at odds with the rest of the local populace; even the smoke from his chimney, as the town's leading merchant cleverly observed, was of an unusual colour. In consequence of all these suspicious peculiarities, the usurer was also known as Ezra the Stranger, and it was under this name that he was penned into the official archives.

Since the death of his wife, Leah, he had become mother as well as devoted father to his only child, Iscah. No commercial transaction, no business involving money, could ever distract the usurer from attending to his only daughter's needs. Although already a blossoming young woman of fifteen, she was still to him an innocent child.

Aside from his one friend, Tull, no one ever visited the usurer. He had no other friends and remarkably few acquaintances; he lived apart, detached.

'Don't talk to me about getting married again,' he would admonish Tull whenever the latter brought up his solitary state. The mere thought of a stepmother for his beloved daughter was enough to bring tears to his eyes.

At night, after young Iscah had gone to bed, the usurer would sit for hours over hot glasses of tea with his friend Tull, studying the scriptures by the flame of an oil lamp, philosophising, meditating, discussing religion, life, and many other things. Although business was never mentioned, Tull knew a great deal about Ezra's trade. He knew, for instance, that the usurer was fond of small, gently-spoken folk. 'Loudmouths have soft brains and stiff fingers,' he would say, 'and the rich are excellent liars.' Comments like this would come to light whenever Ezra reflected on human character, and on the peculiar nature of men, with which he was so conversant.

Tull knew of cases in which his friend had quietly forgone repayment by those who, in bad ventures, had lost his and their own money, and particularly if a sickness or bereavement had struck the debtor's household. And although the usurer dearly longed to be accepted by the members of the town community as one of them (a dream he had inherited from his forefathers), he maintained the strictest secrecy over all his righteous deeds.

A short distance away, on the other side of the street, lived the aforementioned leading merchant, a shipping magnate, who harboured in his bosom a longstanding hatred toward the usurer. Apparently this had something to do with their past, some incident the usurer could not forget and the merchant could not afford to remember. As it happened, the shipping magnate had an agent, Enzo, an exceptionally good-looking young man, a poet and something of a foxy Don Juan, who was familiar with the corporeal geography of the town's every maiden. One day the magnate had a word in his agent's ear, and in no time at all Enzo had wormed his way into Iscah's craving heart.

They met in secret, in a lonely park on the other side of town. There, amid the green rustle of leafy shrubs, Enzo the poet lulled his willing inamorata in his strong arms. 'Iscah, my love,' he intoned, 'my one and only flame. Let my storm come into thee, in my God's and my honour's name.' And she, the lesser poet, answered him: 'I will your storm of love appease; and for your God, I'll crawl on bleeding knees.' Enzo, flushed with his success, asked Iscah to meet with him that very night, and promised her that she would feast her body and her soul on the manifold arts of love bestowed upon him by Eros himself.

They eloped at midnight. But first, held fast in Enzo's irresistible spell, Iscah emptied her father's house of every piece of jewellery, every golden ducat she could lay her hands on. As she was leaving she scribbled a hasty note. When the usurer awoke next morning and discovered his daughter gone, he broke down and wept. 'How could she do this?' he lamented. 'My only child, my precious Iscah, how?'

He was shaken from his lamentations by a knock on the door. His heart jumped – yes yes, she has come back. She has realised her grave mistake and returned to her home, her loving nest. It is but human to err, and equally human to forgive... Ezra the usurer was ready to forgive; already he had forgiven. Joyfully he ran to fling open the door.

In the entrance stood the magnate, in the company of two policemen.

'What, what ... why are you here?' cried the bewildered usurer. 'Has anything, God forbid, happened to my daughter?'

'We know nothing of that,' the two officers carolled in unison. 'We only know that we have orders to arrest you.'

'Arrest me? Why? On what charge?'

'Possessing stolen goods,' replied the magnate with a smirk.

Ezra was dumbfounded. 'It's a lie,' he cried, 'a blatant lie. All my goods are bought with my own money. I can swear to that, on the Holy Bible.'

'We'll see,' said the magnate.

The court proceedings were arranged without delay. The magnate, thanks to Enzo's skills in the art of love, was able to produce a list of eighteen valuable items in the usurer's possession, all of which the latter had allegedly stolen. His daughter's signature appeared at the foot of the statement, and the young agent verified the allegations in every detail.

'What do you say now?' asked the Doge, who was presiding as judge over the trial. 'Your own future son-in-law has testified under oath against you. Do you still insist on pleading your innocence?'

After a pause, the usurer replied, 'Your honour, my daughter would never marry a liar.'

A sudden silence descended on the courtroom. Even the Doge was momentarily taken aback. He quickly regained his composure, and his rasping voice rang out through the chamber once again. 'Let the defendant remain upstanding,' he declared. 'I am about to pronounce judgment.'

He cleared his throat theatrically. 'This is one of the most astonishing cases I have ever had brought before me. A pure, innocent maiden, supported by her upright young fiancé, has signed a declaration that unmasks her father's heinous criminality – a parasite who not only made himself rich on the backs of our little folk, but used their hard-earned money, their sweat and blood, to purchase, harbour and resell stolen goods. Usurer, have you anything to say in your defence?'

Ezra did not look up. He remained silent.

'Give this bloodsucker the rope!' screamed the mob from the public gallery. 'Cut the dog to bits!'

The judge held up the palm of his right hand. 'Yes, gentle people, he deserves as much, and our sacred law permits us to exact this punishment. And yet . . . ' he paused to let the din subside. 'And yet, I am about to teach this rascal the true meaning of noble justice. Defendant, you are free to go.'

There was another uproar, greater and fiercer and more menacing than the first. The Doge again lifted his right hand. He looked down upon Ezra, who stood there, uncomprehending. 'Thank you, your honour,' he murmured.

'But wait,' the Doge called out. 'Not yet.'

In the courtroom and the gallery, one could have heard a feather drop.

'In accordance with our time-honoured judicial system,' the judge resumed, 'I hereby decree that one half of everything you possess – house, chattels, jewels and moneys – is, from this moment, the property of our divine state. The other half is to be given over to your daughter and her betrothed. And further, I order you, usurer, in view of our mild sentence, and as an expression of gratitude to our people, especially to our illustrious fellow citizen,' and he bowed towards the magnate, 'I order you, Ezra the Strange, that you must, under peril of your life, once and forever renounce your abominable faith.'

That night the usurer slept in the street, sheltering under a tree on a vacant block of land. He sat with ash on his head, bewailing the loss of his daughter, cursing the day of his birth. 'Oh, why, why, *why*, my God, have You impregnated my life with such disaster? They have cut so deep, so deep into my poor heart; they have cut off my arm, right up to the shoulder-blade.' His friend Tull had heard his cries and came to offer him comfort. Ezra pushed him aside. 'No, Tull, don't open your mouth, don't even try. Words will offend. But oh, it is so cold, so icy cold. Cover me, Tull, cover me with whatever you have. It won't be long now, I know, it won't be long.' And then for the first time he looked up at Tull. 'Will you do something for me, my loyal friend?' he said.

Tull nodded, stroking the usurer's brow.

'If you see Iscah, give her this locket – it contains a picture of her mother. Tell her that everything I had, everything I ever worked for, was for her. And tell her that I have not stopped loving her.'

As the new day arrived on the eastern horizon, the usurer expired. Tull gave him a customary burial, recited *Kaddish*, and left.

It is now more than four hundred years since God had mercy on our usurer's soul. Yet he is not forgotten. For through all those years, there has not been a single tempestuous night when Ezra the usurer did not re-emerge from his grave to prowl the deserted streets of his town. A demented phantom, he roams the canals and bridges, howling wildly into the merciless dark.

BUG'S EDEN

In a neglected paddock, obscured from human observation by rampant weeds, in a pathetic pile of composted rubbish, old rags, and broken bottles half-covered by loose soil and rotting straw, lived a tribe of cunning bugs. Out of sight, as if on a forgotten island, these creatures multiplied in an ideal environment and had great joy of their world.

The more rubbish that was dumped in this field, the more congenial it became for its inhabitants. Rubbish provided a medium in which they flourished, breathing free and benefiting undisturbed from nature's bountiful space. With their bug psychology, they understood that the more rubbish and the more weeds, the better obscured they would be – and the less likely it was that any human eye would detect them.

As is the case in all societies, these bugs had their distinctive social order. They had their leaders, even their distinguished families, and, according to an ancient but rigidly observed constitution, knew precisely what was forbidden and what was allowed. They lived an orderly existence according to the laws that governed their grubby lives.

It was a black sin to breach any of these laws. Even so seemingly trivial an offence as failure to join the rest of the tribe in its communal puddle-bath was strictly punished. There was no negotiation. Any attempt to stray from the established procedures as laid down by the most important beetles meant ostracism, isolation and, in the worst cases, death. To reduce the risk of violations, every precedent had been carefully enshrined in the official chronicles. On special occasions, these chronicles were publicly recited as a warning to the younger generation.

One strange characteristic of the inhabitants of this community was that they always crawled backwards. At least, outside observers might understandably have thought it strange. The bugs, however, were of a different opinion. They found it quite normal to move in this way and derided all those freakish species that progressed in the opposite manner.

If a cabbage-white should stroll over a bare rock in the paddock, the bugs would be seized by hysterical gales of laughter at the sight. How fortunate was the offending butterfly to have wings, so that it could flutter off and leave that dark little world. Among the bugs, forward movement meant public shaming and exile, in accordance with the code.

It was a quiet backwater, this bug's eden. As in any society, there was birth and mating and death. Its members had their preferences and their antipathies – naturally, more tensions than affections, as tends to be the general rule. It only needed to be rumoured that someone had collected a little more compost than was customary and the fortunate one would be assailed with envy, hostility and abuse. He would be denounced as dishonest, dishonourable and ill-bred.

Early one bright morning, a loud roaring was heard: a clangour of metal tools and human voices. The brown tribe had forebodings of disaster. And so it befell.

Heavy boots stomped across the fields. Sharp steel tines ripped up the weeds without mercy. Spades dug deep and turned the topsoil of this previously neglected land.

A great terror seized the inhabitants. They scurried about in panic (backwards, of course) but no one knew where to go.

They fled in all directions hoping to save their pathetic lives. Naturally, the first to flee were the VIBs. As is usual in these situations, they availed themselves of all the excuses normally made by such luminaries.

In the confusion, no one was spared. Insults were traded, petty officials rudely contradicted their elders and superiors. It is said that some came to blows. That may have a rather fanciful ring, but in chaos all is possible.

By evening, this former brown paradise resembled the field of slaughter after a battle. There was no remaining sign of weeds, no old rags or broken bottles, merely a well-turned soil. The field was divided by straight furrows in which slaughtered grubs lay in their thousands. A gentle breeze soon buried them under a film of dust.

The bright spring weather brought green shoots and white smiling flowers which, in their brave youthfulness, dared look directly at the sun. Earnestly and full of concern, the gardener watched his blossoming crop. He knew only too well that deep under the surface, where they could not be observed, there survived a feverishly active remnant of the once-thriving community.

The survivors were indeed busy, and relentless. With thin poisoned little members, they attacked the immature roots that nourished the delicate life of the flowers. Oh, how cunningly they waited until the roots grew a little bigger. Then they set to work like parasites and built nests that were fed by the luckless plants. The gardener could see nothing because they remained under the surface, but he knew what was happening. Wherever he spotted a crooked stalk, a wilted plant with an overgrown flower-head, he knew that the bugs were at work.

Impotent and bitter at heart, he observed his garden. 'Oh God! What can I do?' he said.

At the same time he understood that there are creatures which live under the earth and are a part of it. Could one then change the nature of the whole world? And perhaps, he thought apprehensively, the plants even loved those bugs...

But the underground tribe had no time for thought. They didn't hesitate. They didn't stop, even for one moment, their poisonous war with the garden. Oh, how well they knew that the gardener would eventually grow weary. And then, as soon as he rested, as soon as he began to rely on faith alone, they would rise up and lay waste the land he was so zealously cultivating.

Soon after that, the weeds would again return. The pretty blossoms and the delicate grasses would be overwhelmed. The brown beetles would once more push through the flimsy surface and once more, with renewed energy, re-establish their bug's eden.

HANS THE FIDDLER

Alfred Berg was a well-known antique dealer in Vienna. He was the eldest son of a converted Jew called Moishe Salzberg, who had come from a small Galician town in the last quarter of the nineteenth century. Alfred's early involvement with antiques was obscure and, according to his rivals, a little shady. But any embarrassing antecedents had been forgotten by 1914, when a son, Hans, was born to Alfred and his wife Matilda. By then Alfred was one of the best-regarded merchants in the trade, a respected member of his local Catholic church, and president of the parish council.

Hans was born at the start of the Great War and grew up with little concern for family origins. His sole passion was music. But he was proud of his Uncle Willi, who had lost an arm and won an Iron Cross at the front. In fact, there was no limit to his admiration for Uncle Willi. It was a great honour, on Sundays, to stroll Vienna's main promenade, where the young ladies would admire his charming, heroic uncle.

The boy was a born musician and quickly fulfilled his early promise. Hans loved his violin with a sensual, almost jealous passion. Whenever he entered a concert hall for a recital, people would remark that he walked like a priest of music holding in his arms a holy scroll of sound.

The Bergs were respectable citizens, respected by their neighbours. There was no question of their patriotism. Nevertheless, with the first appearance of Nazism on the Vienna scene, Alfred cannily decided to invest a little in the new cause – for security's sake. You never knew what might happen. One should be prepared for all eventualities.

This new cause was enthusiastically embraced by the family. When Hans was appointed first violin to the Vienna Symphony Orchestra, his parents gave him a golden swastika to wear in his lapel. Everyone, even the dull-witted Willi, felt this to be another astute step in the family's establishment. Adjusting to the times had been a family tradition since the Salzberg days.

The year 1934 was one of love and struggle for Hans. He voluntarily enlisted in the militia, which was so active in suppressing the Schutzbund. And he fell in love with Gretchen, of the peaches-and-cream complexion. They married two years later.

The wedding was an impressive event. Gretchen came from old wealth and the braid of her family's powerful military connections was well represented. There was a field of elegant ladies, perfumed blossoms among whom Willi fluttered with his one pinned-up sleeve like an injured but illustrious butterfly.

And then came that fateful day in 1938 when the Germans annexed Austria. The populace was overjoyed. It was grand to be members of a Greater German Race. Only the day before, young Hans had learnt that his Gretchen was pregnant. He was chuffed with pride and patriotism.

Meanwhile, old Alfred, who held himself to be something of a philosopher, insisted to all who would listen: 'Today a man, especially an Austrian, is obliged to heed the summons of History. Our destiny beckons to a glorious future. And the essence – aha! the essence,' he would nod prophetically, 'is to understand that the drama now being played out on the streets of Vienna is clearly an historical necessity; a logically necessary emergence of the generations-old conflict which we (thanks only to the wise foresight of our father's conversion) chose to avoid.' And he would conclude: 'He who does not wish to get caught up in the conflict must, on purely patriotic grounds, remain silent, silent, and once more silent.'

Even so, the outbreak of war brought great changes to the lives of the Bergs. Hans, a member of the militia, was mobilised into the army. His beloved Gretchen packed his things, and he bade farewell to his family. His father was swollen with pride. Gretchen carefully pinned the golden swastika to Hans's lapel, and off he went.

One can perhaps imagine the scene at the Bergs' when, an hour later, Hans was back again, standing pathetically in the doorway of his home. Alfred Berg, indignant, was the first to speak. 'What outrage is this?' he thundered. 'Do you think a man who is about to become a father can betray his nation?'

Had Hans been able to bring himself to it, he would have swiped his father on the jaw. But that was not their way. In keeping with his upbringing he heard his father out, before mumbling: 'They told me they don't need my sort, and if they ever wish to deal with me they'll know where to find me.' And that was how things turned out.

By mid-1941, Germany was feverish with the excitement of its many great military triumphs. It was the supper hour and Alfred's wife, Matilda, had just set the table. Suddenly, without warning, there was a pounding on the front door. Before Alfred had time to open it, the door was smashed in, and on the threshold stood two black-uniformed members of the SS.

'You will pardon our dramatic entry,' they announced as if the words had been rehearsed. 'We are not certain that the people we are after live here. We are looking for the sons of that old Jewish swindler Moses Salzberg. One of them is called Alfred. We don't have the other's name, but we know that the Jewish louse shot himself in the arm to avoid conscription during the last war.'

Willi sprang at them with his one fist raised. But the visitors seemed quite prepared for such unruly, provocative Jewish behaviour. Six more armed men rushed into the apartment. The whole family was beaten severely. Alfred, Willi and Hans were dragged off, to the applause of their neighbours.

The battered Matilda whispered to Gretchen that she should run quickly to her father for help. Then she put on her best hat and went to the priest whose loyal devotee Alfred had been for so many years. The priest was standing before the altar, his arms spread cruciform. He told her that it must be God's will, God's will, and quickly withdrew. Matilda's lifelong respect for the cloth kept her silent. Perhaps it *was* God's will. But when she returned home to the news that Gretchen's father, too, had told his daughter that the fate of Christian Europe was at stake and his hands were tied, Matilda let out a bitter groan.

During the last days of August 1944, Hans, his Gretchen and their four-year-old Willi arrived in Auschwitz. In accordance with Nazi logic, because the pretty young woman was holding the little boy's hand tightly in hers, they were both sent to their death. Hans, however, thanks to his fiddle, joined the Dead Symphony of camp life. He was appointed musical director.

It was here that Hans became acquainted with David, a flautist from Prague, who introduced him to a Jewishness he had never before encountered. For David behaved as if imbued with an inner freedom which could not be taken away from him, no matter what. He radiated a true dignity of spirit – and a genuine pride in being a Jew.

One day in late December, while the camp's other inhabitants huddled together like sheep for a little warmth as frost and falling snow pierced their bones with cold, Hans and his orchestra waited in a large hall in the main barracks of the SS. A Christmas tree decorated with paper angels stood in one corner. In the centre of the room was a long table decked out with food and drink. The SS hierarchy sat around it with godlike arrogance. The Jewish inmates served them, fearfully attentive to their every movement.

The camp chaplain delivered a sermon about the ages-old Jewish criminality. God had sent the Germans to rectify things. When the chaplain had finished he fluttered his pudgy white hands at the orchestra and called: 'Prisoners – begin!'

What happened at this point could not have been expected by anyone in the whole camp. Hans hurled his fiddle to the ground in front of him, stepped forward and stamped upon it.

Almost instantly, the head *kapo* rushed up and slammed him in the chest with an iron bludgeon. Blood spurting from his mouth and nose, Hans fell prostrate.

A deathly silence blanketed the hall.

The tension was relieved by the chaplain. He did not want to spoil a holy feast. With careful tread and a swishing of his cassock, he approached the orchestra. He stepped over Hans's body, gestured once more with his delicate hand, and proceeded to conduct a chorus of 'Silent Night'.

Later, back in the barracks, Hans lay cradled in the flautist's arms. He gazed up into his friend's face and managed a feeble smile. 'David, David,' he said with his dying breath. 'What a lucky man you are.'

YASHKA

Thomas Weiss and his Austrian-born parents, Fritz and Gertrude Weiss, alias Fishel and Gittel Weisenberger, well-known European silk manufacturers, arrived in Australia from Vienna in 1947. Thomas was a spongy lad of fifteen: exceptionally bright, good-looking, well-spoken and well-behaved – but a little cynical, with a touch of self-hatred.

At school he excelled in all subjects; but because he dreamt of being a writer, mastery of the English language became not only his major discipline but his ongoing daily obsession. By the time he reached university, Thomas's diction was a veritable song of eloquence.

Like not a few other Jewish immigrants, Thomas also craved to blend in. In this regard he was up against several obstacles: his semitic features, his bourgeois mannerisms and, ironically, his artful English – which, although it made him a favourite with the professors, became a slight barrier to his ambition of reinventing himself and dissolving into the assimilatory river of university life. To counterbalance these drawbacks, Thomas consciously avoided all contact with Jewish students, their campus organisations and their activities.

But, as an old Yiddish saying tells us, a man thinks and God sings. This is where Yashka comes into the picture. There wasn't a male student in the whole university who was not in love with the beautiful, blue-eyed, brilliant freshman from the faculty of creative arts, the charismatic Yashka Jaronski. One day a fellow student by the name of Sam Silberberg, to whom Thomas had taken an instant dislike from day one, stopped him and declared: 'You know, mate, I'd give my right arm to go out with Yashka, but it seems she's only got eyes for you.'

'I should be so lucky,' Thomas retorted brusquely, and quickly vanished into his next class.

Every story has a life of its own, and every life has its own story. A few days later, in the union cafeteria, Yashka walked in, spotted Thomas, came up to his table and, without any preliminaries, announced: 'At last we can have coffee together. And one of these days, maybe even dinner. What do you say, Thomas?'

'Y-yes, have a seat, by all means,' stuttered the master of words. He quickly regained his composure and, like a bewitched little boy eyeing a long-promised gift, fixed his gold-rimmed gaze on the beautiful and brilliant Yashka's fulsome lips.

In the manner of a hurricane that, without warning, assails a drowsing virgin island, Yashka burst into Thomas's life. At first he hardly knew what had hit him, and he walked about the campus as though under a spell. Suddenly, his classes were too long, the lecturers were bores, his watch crawled too slowly; nothing made sense – except when he was caught within the storm of their lovemaking. Spending the night with *his* Yashka was, to Thomas, tantamount to ownership of the hanging gardens of Babylon and all the other wonders of the world.

So here he was, the envy of all, a bright future in literature ahead of him; and his love, charming, clever, and beautiful as a fresh spring breeze – what a hand life had dealt him. And there they were, evenings in the coffee-shops leaning into each other over glasses of red wine and flickering candles, drinking from the depth of each other's eyes. How could they know that the powdery wings of the moth scorched by the candle-flame were trying to tell them something?

For as in many such cases, these two young and passionate lovers – who knew so little about each other's past – were ignorant of the fact that a single night, a single hour, sometimes even a single look, can shape one's entire future. Already, in the darkness of their bliss, they had taken their first bold strides into the unknown.

On one of these coffee-house evenings Yashka, quite nonchalantly, said to him: 'Thomas, you're Jewish, aren't you?'

'Does it make a difference?' he replied, alarmed.

'Yes, a great deal – because you see, I'm Jewish too.'

Thomas was astounded. 'But – you look so... And your *name*... Yashka, you're having me on!'

So she told him about her history. Her grandfather Jozef Jaronski had been a convert to Judaism, and had gone to the gas chambers with the other millions. According to her father, a leading member of the Jewish community in London (where he was still living), Jozef could have saved himself had he been willing to deny that he was Jewish; but that was not his way, nor his son's – nor Yashka's either, she was quick to add. She explained that she was not religiously observant, just consciously and resolutely Jewish. It was her answer to the evils that had been inflicted on her people.

Thomas was dismayed. He, who had so wanted to blend in, to be the same, could not come to grips with having fallen hopelessly in love with someone so fiercely *other*. It was what he had evaded all his life, and now he found himself trapped after all. But it was too late to withdraw, he had unwittingly crossed his personal Rubicon. Ah well, love always wins through, he thought.

One evening four years later, Thomas is feeling particularly dejected. He paces up and down, he purses his lips just like his father did whenever he retold how he had been thrown out of his own factory. Thomas and Yashka have been living together for some months now. She is already a successful travel consultant; he a part-time lecturer and writer. But something is gnawing at Thomas's heart. He cannot cope with the way of life Yashka has chosen for herself, for *them*. Her blessing over the candles on Friday nights is a medieval custom. And there is the kosher kitchen, with its absurd segregation of meat and dairy foods; and the strange sights and sounds in the synagogue on the High Holy Days; and Yashka's unexpected involvement in Jewish community affairs. All this and more has been eating away at his spirit, he feels caged; yet somehow the expert linguist is unable to voice his feelings.

So Thomas skirts the issue. 'You know, Yashka,' he begins, 'I had another unpleasant encounter today with that dreadful huckster Silberberg.'

'Why do you say that? He seems a decent enough man,' Yashka responds. 'It's not by any chance because Silberberg reminds you that you were once a Weisenberger? I remember how passionately you argued with him when he dropped by last year – "I'm a writer who happens to be Jewish," you insisted.'

This rattles Thomas even more. 'Why bring that up now?' he says.

'Well, it did strike me, at the time, as a bit ... disingenuous. I mean, can you imagine Kafka thinking of himself as a writer who is just *accidentally* a Jew? Or Chekhov declaring he was a writer who merely *happened* to be Russian!'

'Come on, Yashka, now you're carrying things too far.'

'Why, Thomas? Because Chekhov's ancestors pitched their tents in Taganrog, and Kafka's in eternity? Because Chekhov was born in his own country and wrote in his own language, while Kafka was a product of exile? Well, my love, true writers are forever in exile – not only in their own homeland but in their very skin.'

'That, Yashka, is just another romantic myth.'

'Maybe,' she replies. 'But it happens to be true. The feeling of being an exile is at the heart of what is best in literature.'

One night, not long after this almost heated exchange, Yashka whispered to Thomas the news that he was going to become a father. Her lover's reaction was not quite what she had expected.

'What?' shouted Thomas, jumping back abruptly. 'At such a time? No!'

'So what would you like me to do, darling? You know I could never have an abortion. I think we'll need to get married, and very soon. My child must be born in wedlock, and according to the laws of our forefathers.'

'Yashka, I can't agree. It's too soon for us to have a child.' He sighed. 'Look, I'm worn out, I need to get some sleep. We'll straighten it all out in the morning.'

At breakfast it was Yashka who broke the frosty silence. 'Tom,' she stated brightly, 'I've thought of a solution.'

Thomas was visibly relieved. 'Darling, I'm glad you understand that I'm just not ready for parenthood at the moment. We'll do what needs to be done now, and we can have a baby in, say, five years' time. And I promise I'll make an excellent father.'

Yashka winced and shook her head. 'Thomas, that's not what I meant.'

'What, then?'

'We marry now, this very week. And we divorce soon after the baby's born. I want our child to be born within the law… Maybe, for both of us, to live apart would be the best solution.'

'Yashka, how could I ever agree to that?' cried Thomas. 'I couldn't live without you, not any more. You're everything to me.'

But Yashka, although she loved Thomas dearly, knew that this was not a time for weakness. Through streaming tears she whispered, 'Tom, I think it was all a mistake. Perhaps we really don't belong together after all.'

Thomas was beside himself. 'No, no, Yashka, how can you say that? You know we do! And to prove it, I'm ready this minute – despite my feeling that a baby now could spell disaster for us – I'm ready this very minute to go with you to a celebrant.'

'Not a celebrant, Thomas. A rabbi. And yes, right now, today. There's no time to lose.'

Yashka gave birth to a healthy boy, whom they named Joseph, after her grandfather. Thomas was overjoyed, though there was one little hiccup. He had settled on a particular doctor for the circumcision, but Yashka insisted on a religious professional in the presence of a *minyan*. She got her way. As always.

After six months Yashka returned to work – her income was needed to keep the household afloat. Thomas was earning close to nothing. Obviously, to become a writer one needed more than just a talent for language. In the wake of his third unsuccessful novel he turned to writing reviews and criticism, for which he at least received some payment. He also tried his hand at feature articles for the newspapers. But although he worked hard, his earnings remained meagre. Yashka knew that he was suffering, could see how his pride was hurt and how morbid he had become. She feared that their marriage was in jeopardy, but she loved the father of her child more than ever and did everything she could to maintain an equilibrium. Somehow they struggled on.

Prior to his fourth birthday party, little Joseph asked his parents to invite five children – Polly, Victor, Andrew, Ronnie and Jane – with whom he always played at the local kindergarten he attended. One afternoon in late summer, Thomas waited outside the kindergarten gates to make contact with the parents of Joseph's friends and invite them as well. To his astonishment it turned out that, out of a class of some thirty children, his son's friends were all Jewish.

The party was a wonderful affair. Yashka decorated the apartment with colourful balloons and streamers, there was a birthday cake with four candles, and everyone enjoyed the party games. It seemed that the parents all knew each other, and there was much lively chatter about current films and imminent holidays. But Thomas had mixed feelings about these people, who were all from Eastern European backgrounds; not only was he a little jealous of their closeness, but he suspected that, spiritually, Yashka belonged more to them than to him.

When everyone had left, he and his wife sat at the table while Joseph opened his presents. Thomas felt suddenly depressed – even betrayed. 'My four-year-old son,' he said, not quite under his breath, 'is dragging me back into the cursed ghetto.'

His wife looked up, startled. 'No, darling, you're wrong. A ghetto made by gentiles for Jews *is* a curse. But a ghetto made by Jews for Jews – that's a blessing.'

'Such an approach,' Thomas fired back, 'would be totally foreign to *my* people. Where I grew up, a ghetto was a ghetto no matter who engineered it.' He had wound himself up and there was no turning back. 'Sometimes,' he ploughed on, 'even a home can turn into ... an intolerable ghetto!'

Quietly, unexpectedly, Yashka rose from the table and walked towards him. She cradled his head in her hands and pressed it against her bosom.

'Love will see us through,' she whispered. 'With all our ups and downs, all our differences, I never doubted your love. You must never doubt mine... You see, Tom,' she went on, 'where I grew up, you had to grow up quickly. There was no pre-school.'

'There's no pre-school anywhere,' said Thomas, appeased. 'Though I had a good childhood, a fine youth, caring parents, and now...' He took her hands and smiled into her eyes. 'Yashka, the best thing that ever happened to me was you.'

On a Sunday afternoon late in spring, Thomas sits alone on his veranda. Breathing deeply of the moist, freshly-mown grass, he ponders his past. With resignation but no bitterness, he recalls his triumphs, his mistakes, his evasions of an unavoidable reality – his stupid desire to blend in. How happy Yashka would have been, if only he had understood then what he understands now.

Three years ago, after a short illness, death had taken hold of Yashka. The loss had been unbearable. If only...

All of a sudden he hears a voice, from deep within. It is ... Yashka's voice!

Tom, says the voice. *For the sake of my memory, go back to your writing desk. I know you can do it now – you must. I always had faith in you.*

The voice pauses, then resumes. *Tom, listen. Listen to the first line of your novel. Listen to these wise words, spoken long ago by my father.*

At first there is only silence. But slowly the silence forms itself into a sound, and the sound shapes itself into a melody, and within the melody Thomas is certain he can hear words.

Life is a river on a mountain slope. An obstacle may alter its course, its colour, even its music, but never ever arrest its flow...

THE JOURNEY

We met at dusk, on a flight from Melbourne to New York. As I was shown to my seat I spotted the title of the book she was reading: *The Trial* by Franz Kafka. She noticed my smile. Maybe she thought I was a sceptic, for no sooner had we exchanged the usual pleasantries than she asked, rather mischievously, 'You have misgivings about young Franz?'

'Oh, not at all, not at all,' I rushed to reassure her. 'In fact, I am one of his most fervent admirers. In my opinion, Kafka is the greatest of twentieth-century poets.'

She gave me a long and penetrating look, perhaps to ascertain the sincerity of my statement.

'You know,' she said after another moment's hesitation, while her slender, artistic fingers cradled the book like a holy talisman, 'twice a year I travel between New York and Melbourne, and Kafka has always been my best, my most truthful companion.'

'I can understand that,' I replied. 'Because Kafka was not only a great poet, but a profound observer of human character, of the mechanics of human conflict – which places him among the elite of biblical poets.'

She became visibly excited, her face flushed, and for a split second our eyes met in a strange embrace. The plane had just taken off and was making its smooth ascent into the night. Outside hung the inescapable expanse of the dark, blue-velvet firmament, spotted with billions of golden stars, reaching out to other worlds, to other planets in unknown galaxies. I looked out on it all in wonder. An eternal harmonious cosmos, I thought; and yet there are still fools who claim there is no God...

Presently dinner was served. I observed that she ate with a kind of sadness, as if eating for her were a waste of time. I sensed she had a need to talk, to impart a story. She had detected in me an eager listener; obviously the food was a distraction.

But as soon as she finished and pushed away the tray, the book was back in her hands. Once again her sensitive fingers began to leaf nervously through the pages of Kafka's predicament.

After a few minutes she closed the book, held up a tattered bookmark on which some lines were scribbled, and turned towards me. 'Listen to this, I must read you this,' she said, her voice like a whisper of command. 'Listen how this brief description of *The Trial* has epitomised the whole tragic destiny of my people. Joseph K. is accused of something, but he doesn't know of what; he wants to defend himself, but he doesn't know how. He knows that a trial is imminent, but he doesn't know when. And one morning they come, he is arrested and taken to a deserted quarry, where they –' She trailed off, let the bookmark drop. 'Where they brutally murder him!' she hissed. 'Like a dog!'

She paused, took a deep breath, and, as if looking for an escape, sank back into her seat. Then, with what was almost a muffled sob, she said: 'Now you know what they did to my father, to my people, and how Kafka's bleak, prophetic fantasy turned into a nightmare reality.'

The temperature in the plane had dropped, the cabin lights were dimmed. Some of the passengers reached for the woollen blankets provided by the airline and snoozed off into their world of dreams. But we two – we who just hours ago had been perfect strangers – we two, united so unexpectedly by the force of our common destiny, remained very much awake.

'I was born many summers ago,' she began in the tone of a sad storyteller, 'in the land beyond the frozen river, in a large village. I lived with my father in our little house, where you couldn't see the walls for the books. Father was a schoolteacher and taught mathematics at the village school. But in his free time he studied philosophy, especially the ancient Greek masters. I remember him forever complaining, only half-jokingly, about the lack of decent footnotes, which impeded his reading. But he wouldn't give up, giving up was not in his nature.

'I was his only child. Mother died in childbirth. I was brought up by a neighbour, Slava, a humble woman with a homespun generosity. She loved my father like a mother and wife: she cooked our meals, cleaned our house, and at the end of each week, when she changed our linen, she would take a hot bath and, half-naked, would go into father's bedroom and eagerly await his homecoming. No one in the village knew, except for me and Slava's daughter, Sabka, who spied on them through the keyhole. To learn how her mother, fifteen years older than my father, instructed him in the art of rustic lovemaking.

'Father was a respected man in our community. He had a small circle of friends, but none of them were from the same background as ours. On the first Wednesday of every month they used to gather in our house, in the room where you could get drunk on the aroma of old books. They listened to father read and, afterwards, listened to him explain in simple terms the metaphors and hidden meanings so memorably depicted in the Greek legends.

'Our overcrowded village, which was strategically positioned, dreamt of becoming a city. We were the first in the region to be granted electricity and running water, and some of our elders even had a telephone. Our schooling was good, and the inhabitants of the village were upright and humane. Yet, as it turned out, a people can change on the surface, and remain unchanged down below.

'One day war broke out. Things began to go badly for the country beyond the frozen river. The crazy old toothless prophet Medko, who had lived for the past thousand years concealed in the foggy psyche of our villagers, reappeared. Suddenly people began to whisper about night-visits by small white spirits, by laughing ghosts, by evil gnomes and satyrs. No one dared to venture out into the dark. There was talk of an imminent invasion of Cyclops riders who fed their two-headed horses on live children.

'A rumour got about: years ago, in the thick of night, the full moon had transformed a local young maiden into a she-wolf. Her mother had caught her inciting both the Devil and her own father to mount her alternately. Medko had slit the girl's throat, to protect the purity of family life.

'Such a heroic deed increased Medko's stature in the eyes of the once so humane villagers. A few days later, at daybreak, when the *new* Cyclops thundered into our village – not on two-headed horses but on roaring steel tanks – Medko's spectre made its appearance on our doorstep. It was Slava who confronted its new agents, with the sharp edge of her axe, but father gave her a sign to step back. "After all," he said, "I am only being taken in to clarify matters." Like many others of our people, he did not understand – would not have believed – to what wickedness, to what unspeakable evil, man was capable of descending. When Slava learnt what they had done to father, she hanged herself.

'On the advice of a young friend of father's named Vasili, I moved in with Sabka. We slept together in one bed. With her left hand Sabka cradled my head, and in her right her father's loaded gun. At midnight we heard a faint knock on the window-pane. There stood Vasili, father's friend, in his fur coat and cap. His eyes were alight with daring and he looked like an enraged two-legged wolf.

'"Children," he said. "Don't ask any questions. We have no time to lose!"

'The moonless night lay in an ominous silence: one could almost hear the fall of the white snowflakes. With the cunning of an animal sniffing danger Vasili led us, on our skis, through the frozen snowfield and into the heart of the mighty forest.

'Suddenly three men who had been lying in wait pounced upon us. But Vasili was ready. With one powerful swing of his axe he split one of the men in two, then engaged the others in battle, screaming "Run, children, run!" We ran. For our escape young Vasili paid with his life.

'Such was our time. A time of little that was noble, and an abundance of evil. A time when genocide was not the exception but the rule. But we will never forget our Vasilis. They will live on forever in the memory of our people.

'And yet, to me, to enshrine his name is not only to acknowledge a noble deed by a noble person; it is also to recognise the victim's inner need to restore at least some face to a defaced humanity — to find a thread of morality in a world gone mad.

'Fifty years have passed since the murder of my father, of Vasili, and of all my dear ones. And yet, whenever I travel upstate in New York — especially in winter, when the forest makes its stand against the invading snow — I hear amid the happy laughter of young skiers my Vasili's desperate scream, "Run, children, run!"...'

We landed.

The terminal was crowded, the atmosphere oppressive with noise and movement. We collected our luggage and stepped out into the humid night.

'How long are you staying in New York?' she asked.

'Only a few days.'

'Perhaps you can spare an evening and have dinner with us? I live with my two sons, Gershon and Basil, and my adopted sister Sabina. It will be good for them to meet you.' Her artistic fingers slipped a small square of paper into my palm.

For a while we both stood forlorn. There was a tremor in our silence. Over our heads a yellow neon blinked. The occasional droplet of rain only made the humidity more unbearable. We shook hands, and held on to prolong the moment; once again our eyes met in that eerie embrace.

I glanced at the slip of paper she had given me. On it was a phone number, with three words: 'Please come. Helka.'

I smiled at her sadly. She nodded.

Perhaps we didn't know how to part. Or maybe we had embarked on a flight of no return. A journey more real than we ourselves had ever been.

BETRAYED

David was born to the west of the wide Vistula, at an interesting time. He was the eldest child of a family of eight. They all lived together beneath a four-storey building, in a windowless basement which David's mother had christened The Castle; her family she dubbed, naturally enough, The Rothschilds.

The daily life of David's neighbourhood may appear, to some readers, rather outlandish. Even I, who happened to live there, could never work it out. What drove these destitute, hungry people? Pressed into dark dwelling-holes by a system that mocked their misery, how could they dream of a flower or a blade of grass, in a town of brick and stone where a forest of ominous brown factory chimneys kept spitting out tons of thick black smoke to rot their lungs? Yet they kept dreaming, and kept creating – books, art, music, philosophy. And they kept caring, so very much, for a world, and a God, that had shamelessly forgotten them.

When David was about fourteen years old he was apprenticed to a tailor. In accordance with the custom of the time he was bound, for the first two years, to attend to all the domestic needs of the master's household. His working day began at 7 a.m. and ended when he was told that it was time to go home. The first task on his daily agenda was to empty the bucket of night-refuse. He then had to light the stove, settle any child who was crying, make sure there was enough fresh water in the house, keep alive the charcoal in the pressing-irons, and be ready to perform other duties, such as carrying home the provisions and helping out with the week's washing.

There was something singular about David, something oddly contradictory. There was his innocent young face which bespoke a mature knowledge of hardship; and there was his humble background, belied by his dignified, almost proud bearing. No burden of work could ever kill the song within him; he was forever singing – strange, pleading melodies imbued with ancient dreams and folktales, which would rekindle iridescent promises and buried longings in the hearts of his famished listeners.

From the first day of David's apprenticeship, the two skilled workers in the small tailoring establishment took a liking to him – most notably the younger one, who not only introduced him to the 'magic skill of the little golden needle' but also to the slim pamphlets known as the Penny Library which so romantically depicted the legendary lives of the Russian revolutionaries. All at once a new world opened its doors for David, a world of new ideas, new teachings – the theories of Ilyich Lenin, the heroic deeds of the horseman Budenny, and the daring exploits of Joseph Stalin, who overnight became David's adored idol. The boy was quick to learn; in no time he had learnt how to make a good pair of trousers, and also the bitter truth about our troubled world.

Thanks to David's tailoring skills, a pot of hot soup became a daily presence on the family table. Here, however, as will always happen, the joy was to prove transient, and the 'Rothschilds' were soon toppled from this apex of opulence. Because David, through the influence of his enlightened friend, the skilled worker who had taken him under his wing – and even more so through the influence of the slim pamphlets about the romantic lives of the Russian revolutionaries – not only began to part his shiny dark hair in the very centre of his head, grow a moustache and sport a Cossack-style blouse; as well, he joined the ranks of the clandestine, volatile young movement which had set out to transform the world.

One evening late in summer, as the sun was abdicating the horizon and a foreboding silence descended upon the street, so that one could almost hear the shadows shifting; as the fumes that shrouded the factory roofs dispersed for the night, so that the relentless chimneys stood out frozen now, like a forest of brown tombstones in an endless cemetery – David made his way home. Despite the gloomy landscape, he had good reason to feel elated. At noon that day he had received great tidings. He had been chosen to represent his underground cell, known as the Red Front, on the regional committee of the Party. Tonight he was chairing the first talk, and he was ready.

But so too were the security police, who were waiting for him in his own backyard. It took them only a split second to have David handcuffed, and to toss him into the open doors of their Black Maria. One could accuse our security police of many things, but never, ever, of a lack of knowhow. The whole tenement block stood by and, with a great deal of apprehension, witnessed the brutal spectacle. Some of the women wept, others kept hugging and reassuring David's distraught mother.

Of course, everyone in our grey vertical settlement had known that something was not right with their beloved David. They frowned at his constant disappearances, especially before May Day. They shook their heads at the parting of his hair in the very centre of his head, at the moustache, the Cossack shirt, the packets of books he kept bringing to his basement. These were all valid reasons for doubt, for suspicion. But to see David manhandled like the worst of criminals was something that these people, united in their misery, could not stomach. (For this was a time when human life still had meaning.)

I shall never forget the day when David, after five years of re-education in one of the nation's most prestigious prisons – which the state, with great wisdom and foresight, had erected on a swamp – came home. His posture was stooped, his face strangely white, with a pale red blotch on each cheek. He coughed, and after each cough he would discreetly inspect his white handkerchief. There to greet him were the faithful comrades of his cell, a group of about twenty young men and women, each wearing a red scarf fastened with a ring bearing the image of Karl Marx. In a radiant but solemn mood, his friend Pola led him to the head of the table. David threw his arms open in a gesture of embrace. He whispered gently that it was so good to see them all, and this brought tears to the throats of the younger, less hardened fighters. Pola, softly spoken, petite, with a fair complexion and wondrous brown storytelling eyes, spread a clean white cloth over the table and, without fuss, placed upon it a pot of boiled potatoes, a plate of herring and a bottle of crystal-clear vodka. Then the toasts began. As soon as the drinks had warmed the gathering, everyone burst into song:

Fly higher, fly higher, brave eagles,
The sky is no limit for us;
We are the builders of times to come,
The youth of our proud working class.
Our step is certain and strong,
So is our mighty iron fist;
We are led by the Father of Humankind,
Stalin, our sun in the east.

As if in a trance, David slowly rose to his feet and cleared his throat. When he began to speak, I saw how the dim little room was transformed. Suddenly we were in a cave of legendary riders, readying our mounts, fired with the spirit of vengeance. Then we were all surging forward on our valiant steeds, I myself galloping out in front, on a white stallion, my sabre unsheathed, eager to battle for the holy cause...

A frightful thumping on the door wrested me out of my reverie. At that moment, as the security police broke through into our room, I knew that all our aspirations were shattered and that the revolution was lost.

After several years in prison, Pola came back. She was thin, her hair unkempt. Her eyes, deeply recessed now and ringed with black, spoke defiance, determination. That same evening David came home too. Their embrace was that of comrades in love. Lips sank into lips, hands explored in places they had for so long been denied.

I understood nothing of the conversation, which was conducted in fluent Esperanto. (I was still a schoolboy then.) But as Pola kept repeating in her native language the word *betrayal*, it became clear that something very ugly had taken place on the day when our revolution had been abrogated. David seemed terribly upset, and after each mention of the word *betrayal*, he raised his fist and then slammed it down against his thigh with a thud.

When our country fell to the Germans, the security police of our stony town succumbed to an irresistible need to leave their dossiers on all political suspects to their now rightful heirs, the Gestapo. But let us not judge them too harshly. Perhaps they had to; perhaps they were guided by an inner moral need to ensure continuity...

On a cold, crude winter's day in January 1940, as the morning frost sketched headless pigeons on the shivering windowpane and an east-west wind tore our life to shreds, two Gestapo agents in black woollen coats, with little hooked crosses in their lapels, appeared at Pola's door. Pleasantly, they told her distressed four-year-old daughter that her mama was a witch and that she would return in fifty years or so.

Pola had come across David on the transport. After a three-day journey of some 300 kilometres, the train stopped and they, along with its other occupants, were thrown out into an open, desolate field of snow. They were somewhere near the east. Without any deliberation David and Pola decided to cross the border into the homeland of their political dreams. But to their astonishment, when they reached the border the Soviet guards, their own comrades in a cause to which they were ready to give their young lives, arrested them as smugglers and black-marketeers. David's explanations were of no avail. Nor were his political credentials of any help. The guards didn't care that he was a devoted cadre, a member of the regional executive and head of a secret cell, the Red Front; nor that Pola was herself a true believer who had sacrificed her blossoming years for the common struggle. They didn't care that only death awaited the couple if they returned. 'We have enough spies of our own,' the Soviet officer told them gruffly, and forced them to go back to the German side. (The Germans were still the trustiest allies of the Soviets.)

Pola and David were old hands in the underground. They understood that their return journey would be much easier and safer if they separated. So Pola headed home via the south. That was a terrible winter; the fields were buried under mountains of snow, Pola's flesh was frostbitten wherever it was exposed through rents in her clothing. Hungry and alone, she started begging for bread in the villages she passed through. Some people slammed their doors angrily in her face, others would lift an axe. Obviously her kind were despised by the locals. But on one of those impossible winter evenings, when darkness falls like a black boulder and one has nothing more to lose, she stole into a barn, where she hoped to spend the night and rest her weary body. It was her good fortune that the farm was run by a kindly man of her own background, who found her just in time, otherwise she would certainly have frozen to death. After hearing Pola's story the farmer and his wife invited her to stay for the rest of the winter. 'You wouldn't survive trying to pass through the forest on foot,' he said. 'The snow and the wolves would get you.'

Spring came. Does war know about flowers, butterflies, green meadows, lonely children, craving mothers, bitter heartache? What does war know about such things?

Pola parted with gratitude and affection from these good people and once more took to the road. It was broad daylight when she arrived at the district's main railway station. With the confident demeanour of an experienced member of the underground she went straight up to a wagon and hopped aboard. Suddenly, as if from nowhere, a young man in the uniform of the Hitler Youth appeared beside her. He congratulated her on her agility in jumping into the wagon, and in the same spirit detailed her to join a gang unloading sacks of buckwheat from the next car. Pola tried to beg off. 'I haven't seen my child for such a long time,' she pleaded. The response was two hefty slaps across her face. All the stinking children in her country weren't worth one German soldier's meal, he told her. She realised the buckwheat must come first.

It was at this work that Pola, incredibly, met David again. He looked resigned, bowed as he was under the weight of the heavy sacks – which were stencilled with the symbol of his dreams, the red hammer-and-sickle. Surreptitiously, in a way that no one would notice, he was crying. Although, as Pola recalled, David had often insisted that crying was a petit-bourgeois indulgence, she understood him all too well now.

Pola reached home at the end of April. Her eyes were darkened with suffering. Her little girl flew into her arms, and washed her face with hot tears and kisses. Her mother and father wept, but Pola seemed to have a new hardness about her. She looked at everyone, but seemed unable to let a single tear flow. Her throat was blocked, as if a stone was stuck there.

Three weeks later David came home as well. He turned up at our place, sat on the edge of the bed and remained silent. Pola, without a word, proffered him a mug of hot coffee. He took it in his trembling hands, sipped loudly and, with his mouth still about the rim of the mug, mumbled: 'Do you know what they did to us, Pola?'

She didn't answer straight away. Instead she settled herself beside him on the edge of the bed. Then, in a tone barely audible, she whispered: 'I know, David, I know. They betrayed us all. So foully, so foully betrayed us.'

David slowly shook his head. 'The whole world betrayed us. And the chief traitor was the one we called the Father of Human-kind – our idol.'

It was in the early days of September 1944 that I saw my sister Pola for the last time. Her head had been shaved. She wore a loose white shift that clung to her swollen legs. She was stretched out on the electric fence of Auschwitz, finally at rest.

UNCLE HENOKH'S FRIEND

My uncle Henokh, may his dear soul rest in peace, was a wonderful storyteller. One cold wintry night, as a south wind tore his world asunder and a green rain kept drumming on his roof, he positioned himself by the open hearth (so that the flames lit up the furrows on his parchment face), rekindled his old pipe, took a couple of deep puffs, and with closed eyes began to spin a yarn.

Yah, said my uncle Henokh. The sun had gone into hiding, the day had gone its predecessor's way, and a grey veil enveloped the worn-out town. The streets were deserted, all was quiet, so numb that I could almost hear the sighs of the abused downtrodden pavement.

I ventured into the foyer of the three-star city hotel. In one corner, enveloped in a cloud of cigar smoke, sat the porter Rodriguez. He wore a crimson shirt, partly unbuttoned, perhaps to expose his hairy chest, where, suspended from a heavy chain, a golden crucifix dangled. His well-shaped nose supported a pair of dark glasses through which he kept a watchful eye on the world around him, notably on the shapely hotel-owner, in whose delightful generosity he had a vested interest.

Yah, said my uncle Henokh. (He took another puff and gazed for a while into the rings of disappearing smoke before continuing.) It was not the hotel-owner but the porter's conspiratorial wink that decided who was admitted and who was barred entry.

A suggestive silence reigned in the dimly-lit lounge of the city hotel. At small tables covered with red-and-white checked linen (my uncle had a marvellous eye for detail), over glasses filled with sweet intoxicating liquids, assorted couples were seated, mostly middle-aged men with younger women, some little more than girls still in their teens. They huddled over their drinks, leaning intimately towards each other, absorbed in a silent dialogue, a duel of eyes that might provide the prelude to a night's furtive lovemaking.

Yah, said my uncle Henokh. (*Yah* was, in his opinion, the key to any story – no *Yah*, no story.) Sometimes, to enhance the hotel's business, crafty Rodriguez employed the wench Lilith, whose heavy makeup, husky voice and redolent songs became widely renowned.

> *Sing to me, sing to me, my darling,*
> *The passion of your first kiss lied;*
> *The sweet spring of my childhood*
> *Was choked by your lust and died.*
>
> *The moon fell asleep on our pane,*
> *His face so theatrically pale;*
> *Gently he exposed my white breast*
> *And, cradling me, whispered his tale.*
>
> *How innocently did my body obey;*
> *How quickly the dawn turned to grey.*

Suddenly I thought I noticed a man I had once known, years ago. He sat alone, supporting his balding head with his hand, staring with wide-open eyes into the bottom of an empty glass. *Yah*, it was definitely Amos! He had been such a well-to-do gentleman, married with two young children, as I recalled; and here he was, despondent, shabbily dressed and dirty as a beggar.

I approached his corner and waited. It took him several moments to look up, and a few more to recognise me. 'Ah, Henokh, isn't it?' he said eventually. 'Nice to see you.'

'Yes, and you're Amos,' I replied. 'It must be at least ten years.'

He nodded without enthusiasm.

'But – forgive me for asking – what has happened? You look very different from the last time I saw you. I remember you used to be so sharp and debonair. Everyone admired you, and with good reason.'

Amos drew a deep sigh. 'Why don't you sit down and join me for a while.' His hand swept over the table in a grand gesture of hospitality that belied his demeanour. 'I need to talk – to talk to someone.'

I eased myself into the only other chair at his table, and Amos at once receded into silence. *Yah*, but I knew he was just marshalling his thoughts, probing for a place to start. I ordered two double shots of vodka.

'You know, Henokh,' he began, after downing his drink in one gulp, 'I came to this country penniless, without a profession, without a language, no relatives, no friends, just a very pregnant young wife. But I did well – very well. So people kept patting me on the shoulder and telling me, *Amos, you've arrived, you really have arrived*. How foolish they were. No one ever *arrives*, no one. Every morning, every hour, each human being embarks on an unknown journey.'

Yah, Amos was a well-read man, he loved to philosophise. As the old saying goes, he was an expert in the small letters of the holy scriptures. But I must let him speak for himself, because at this point he started to dig deeper into his past.

'The war,' he resumed, 'came to an end in the spring of 1945. I was forty and had been away from home for four years. The yearning to embrace my wife again occupied my thoughts to the point of hallucination, and there was also my little boy, only two years old when I'd seen him last; I wondered if he would still remember me. And what about my parents, siblings, friends — my God, a whole world I had left behind was now awaiting me.

'It was with the first cry of the rooster that I walked into the township of my birth. The place was still sunk in sleep and a strange silence hovered in the air. The new sunrise was like a resolute whisper, and everything in me began to sing, to laugh, to weep. I was back, back home to my wife and child, to the earth where I was born. Back to the luscious grass sprinkled with yellow wildflowers, the little brook, my beloved forest of silver birches that had protected my soul from freezing during the long nights of the Russian winter.

'I hasten my pace. One more step, one more, and there is my house, my home. Soon, soon I will see my wife, she awaits me with open arms; and my little boy, standing there by her side. The tension became unbearable, my heart was pounding. I thought I would expire at any moment. I knocked, and heard footsteps coming towards the door. It opened.

'It was Tadzik, the town clerk. I recognised my old dressing-gown draped loosely across his bulk. The man gazed at me with a mixture of caution and contempt. "It's you," he said at last. "Don't tell me you're still alive! What on earth are you doing here?"

'And you know, Henokh, I really didn't have an answer. But in that split second I understood. I realised that I was standing in front of my house which had always been my home, and which had never been my home.'

Amos stopped and began to trace circular patterns on the table with his empty glass. *Yah*, he looked so dejected that I didn't know quite what to say, so I told him to go on. Which he seemed willing enough to do.

'I found shelter with the schoolteacher Stefana, whose husband Pawel had been my friend and comrade-in-arms, for we had served in the same regiment and fought shoulder to shoulder at the river Warta trying to repel the invading enemy. Pawel was a valiant fighter who had refused to retreat and had fallen in battle. Stefana had never got over the loss.

'That evening, as I was about to turn in, she came up close to me with a fearful look in her eyes. "Amos," she whispered, "you remember Józek Siekera? He and his gang are back. You have to be careful – don't even show your face in the street."

'"But why, Stefana?" I said to her. "The war is over."

'"It is," she replied, "but not for us. You remember Leizer the tailor. He came back from camp one night last week, to claim his sewing-machine. Next morning they found his headless body."'

Amos nodded sadly. 'After that I lay awake all night, listening to the dark. At around two o'clock I heard a faint knocking. I sprang out of bed, ready to flee (I hadn't bothered to remove my clothes), but before I had a chance to gather my few belongings, the door opened and there stood Stefana, accompanied by a figure whose features I couldn't make out in the dark. "You have a visitor," Stefana whispered, and withdrew.'

Yah, for the first time I noticed a spark in Amos's eye. He nodded again, as if to confirm in advance what he was about to tell me.

'It was Rachel,' he said at last, 'daughter of Yankel the slaughterer. When I'd left home she was only an awkward girl of fourteen. Now she stood before me a full-grown and beautiful young woman. But her eyes were clouded with distress.

' "Rachel, is it really you? Where did you come from, and in the middle of the night?"

' "I live in the attic just above," she answered, pointing upwards. "It has no windows and no doors. Stefana has hidden me here for four years. Food and books she has passed up to me through a trapdoor in the ceiling, but only at night. Stefana always feared our neighbours more than she feared the occupiers."

'I stared at this strange and familiar girl. "Rachel, tell me," I said. "What happened here? What happened to my wife, my boy, my parents, my friends? What happened to the whole town? Where did all our people go?"

' "Amos, it is impossible to describe what took place here," she replied, her sad eyes brimming with tears. "It started with words, strange words, but soon the words took on their terrible meanings. *Sonderkommando*, *ghetto*, *resettlement*, *transport*. And then the sounds – the dogs, the gunfire, the whistle of trains, the whistle of trains, the whistle..." She kept repeating the phrase over and over, and then she fell into me, sobbing. "Amos, we are the only two living Jews left in this town, maybe even in the whole country! They murdered us all!"

'Suddenly she pulled herself away, wiped at her eyes with both hands, and fixed her dark gaze upon me. "Amos," she said, "there is no future for us here. Stefana can't continue to hide me and feed me much longer – it puts her in great danger, and she doesn't have much for herself. I gave her everything I possessed, all the money I had, some family jewellery I'd managed to hold on to. Not that she ever asked for anything, but it was the only way I could express my gratitude."

'She paused then. "But one thing more, Amos. Remember what I just told you. We are the only two survivors of our community. And I am the only witness, but without a witness. There-

101

fore," Rachel's voice took on a sudden resolve. "Therefore, before we leave this room, you have to make me your wife."

'I was astonished. Even as a child, she had never been one for mincing words; but this was beyond belief. "Rachel," I answered slowly. "Think what you are saying. I am twice your age, you could be my daughter..."

'"In that case, Amos," and she smiled for the first time, "I'll do what Lot's daughters did."

'I shook my head. "Rachel, that was ... different, you must see that!..."

'But she was not to be deterred. "*A man whose wisdom exceeds his deeds*," she said, "*can be compared to a tree whose branches are many but whose roots are few.*" Was Rachel really quoting at me from *Pirkei Avoth*, the Ethics of our Fathers? "And besides," she added, "the so-called sin I'm proposing is, in our circumstances, holier than a thousand righteous deeds."'

Yah, Amos placed a bony hand on my wrist. 'You see, Henokh,' he said, 'Rachel's father, Yankel the slaughterer, was not only a man of great piety but of profound erudition. I remember him saying that our people had tertiary education when the others didn't even know about kindergarten. The *cheder*, our primary school; the *Talmud-Torah*, our high school; and the *yeshivah*, our university. Yankel ran an open house of learning, young students were always coming in and out. And contrary to the practice then, he not only allowed but positively encouraged his Rachel to become, in his words, a sweet grape on the biblical vine.

'Anyway, there I was, and there was Rachel. She took my hand and squeezed it, and her warmth flooded my being. "Amos, did it never occur to you," she said, "that at fourteen I was already madly in love with you?" I think I tried to shake my head, to deny any such knowledge, but all at once the room was filled with the pale aroma of an approaching twilight. Rachel's breasts were swollen with longing, her body was sleek and giving. She was not experienced, yet as soon as we began threading loneliness into loneliness, she would not stop until the moon, exhausted, faded into the grey of dawn. Stefana obviously understood, because before she left for work she placed our breakfast – together with Rachel's money and all her family jewellery – on a tray outside the door. A short note read: *Rachel, all this belongs to you. Thank you for giving me the chance to be human.'*

What do you think of that, said my uncle Henokh. Quite a story, eh? (He cleared his throat, puffed a few times on his cooling pipe.) But let me tell you, Amos's story was only just beginning. *Yah*, he pressed my wrist again, and I noticed how animated his features had become. He shifted in his chair, as if to signify the start of a fresh chapter. And so it was.

'Two weeks after our arrival in this lucky land,' he went on, 'Rachel gave birth to twins, a boy and a girl. The girl she named after her mother Michal, and the boy after my father David. "You see, Amos," she told me with an ironic smile, "God has rewarded us better than his faithful Job."

'Rachel blossomed, she became more beautiful than ever, her femininity was admired by young and old, her bearing was sublime, her tread had the lightness of a butterfly – in fact, a few of my friends would sometimes refer to her as "that Rachel Butterfly of yours". She picked up the language in no time. At night, after we made love, she would murmur, "Amos, I adore the place we have come to, the people, their kindness. It's a perfect place to raise a family."

'Once the twins began school, she threw herself into study, lectures, symposiums, books and more books, and all this added to her charm. She also began to write. I'll never forget the day Rachel graduated – together with our two children! How proud

I was to see them, all three of them, arm in arm and parading in their academic gowns.'

Amos took a long sip from his glass, which had been discreetly refilled, and paused, perhaps to pick up the train of some lost thought. 'You know, Henokh,' he remarked at last, 'the most fascinating things in life are those you cannot explain.'

He shifted in his chair before continuing. 'It was not long after the graduation that, out of the blue, Rachel, the mother of two grown-up children, began spending time with my son's friends – you know, going to the same parties, joining them on outings...' Amos shook his head slowly, and the smile that appeared on his lips was a bitter one. 'There was this young poet called Bernard. Rachel called him *Byron* – not because of his scribbling but for his melancholic features, his big irresistible Rasputin eyes. It was certainly under his influence that she took to reciting erotic verses, especially from the *Song of Songs*. We might be sitting at the dinner table, or watching a film on television, when she would suddenly burst forth with, "*Oh, give me the kisses of your mouth, for your love is more delightful than wine.*"

'You can imagine, Henokh, how uncomfortable these new habits made me feel. Not that I suspected anything, mind you – how could I? This was my wife, the girl who had loved me since her teens, the woman who had given me two beautiful children. So I remained silent, though the burden of that silence weighed more heavily upon my heart than the silence itself.

'One evening, as the year was drawing to a close, I said to Rachel: "Perhaps we should go away for a week or two, maybe overseas, maybe on a cruise around the islands. I know how much you love the sea. We could listen to the murmur of the waves, and the ocean breezes could breathe new energy into our lives." Rachel's face lit up at this suggestion. "Amos, what a wonderful idea, how marvellous. Let's take the children too, they deserve a break. And of course we mustn't forget Byron, he is so attached to our family."'

Amos shook his head slowly from side to side, his mouth half-open; *yah*, for a moment he resembled one of those side-show clowns, the ones you feed with ping-pong balls. 'Can you believe that, Henokh?' he exclaimed. 'What could I say? The following morning I instructed my office manager to book five first-class tickets on a popular cruise liner, and on the appointed day the five of us arrived to board the ship. For the first few days it really was like a breath of fresh air, and I found myself unwinding, realising how tense I had allowed myself to become over the past months. One evening, with the waves a little choppy, feeling a little off-colour after a generous dinner, I excused myself and retired to our cabin early, leaving Rachel in the company of Bernard and the twins. When I awoke at around two Rachel had not yet returned; in the morning I noticed that her bunk had not been slept in. The five of us met up at break-fast. Rachel smiled and asked me if I felt better; she said she had stayed up so late that she had decided not to disturb me, and had managed to "improvise" a bed for the night. Bernard ordered more coffee; the twins chattered away. That evening, respond-ing to a sudden impulse, I left them early again, pleading sleepi-ness and a headache. The previous night's pattern was repeated: Rachel did not come back to our cabin! During what remained of the cruise, she slept elsewhere on three more nights out of seven. I never ventured to ask her where, because I knew; and I knew with whom.'

Yah, at this point Amos raised his arms in a gesture of resignation. 'But you know what, Henokh,' he whispered. 'I accepted it. She was a young woman, I reasoned with myself, she had simply needed a break from me, a change, a little fling, and now that it was out of her system, everything would be the way it had been before. And for a while she really did seem more affectionate towards me, more attentive. How guilty she must feel, I thought, and my heart went out to her. On my way home from work on the evening of her fortieth birthday, which fell just a few weeks after we returned from the cruise, I bought her a dozen of the most exquisite scarlet roses, as if to tell her that I understood, that everything was all right. I walked briskly and full of hope, inhaling the loveliness of the oncoming night. Rachel was awaiting me on the threshold – how perfect! She wore a dark-blue dress and her eyes were full of light; as she embraced me, I felt that every fibre in her body was pleading for forgiveness.

'At the end of a sumptuous meal, washed down with many glasses of wine, Bernard, who had been invited for dinner in honour of Rachel's birthday, rose to his feet. His face appeared particularly white in the candlelight, whiter than the sheet of paper from which he began to recite with zeal, but with a tremor in his voice:

Fly with me, love, to the east,
Together we can waken the day,
Rekindle the morning sun
That sleeps behind the silvery grey.
I am young and awkward in love,
Fly with me and teach me, my dove.

'"Bravo, bravo!" shouted our son David. "Hey Bernard, you must be in love." Our daughter Michal echoed him. "Definitely," she said. Rachel got up, walked over to her young friend, and kissed him on the cheek. "Byron, that was beautiful," she whispered. To dispel my unease, I produced from my pocket the antique bracelet I had prepared as a gift for the occasion, and without a word I wrapped it around Rachel's wrist.

'"Oh, Amos," she squealed, "how exquisite, and how very exotic. Thank you so much. It must be incredibly old!"

'"Well, if I were to believe the dealer who sold it to me, this is the very bracelet that Mark Antony presented to Cleopatra on the night of their nuptials!"

'Later, after Bernard and the twins had left and we were about to turn in, Rachel said to me, "Amos, that was such an extravagant gift. You must have spent an absolute fortune!" I stroked her soft cheek. "Nothing," I replied, "is too extravagant if it's for you."

'By the time we went to bed it was long past midnight. It was a night without sleep, but for all the wrong reasons. Rachel lay next to me, numb, withdrawn, cold as a grave. After several attempts to kiss her, to embrace her, to *caress* her even, I sat up in our bed and turned on the light. "What is it, Rachel?" I asked my wife. "What is it that's upsetting you? What has happened? Rachel, tell me, please. What can I do, what is it you want? Tell me, I won't refuse."

'She turned towards me, brushing a strand of hair from her brow. "All right, Amos," said my Rachel who never minced words. "I want a divorce."

'Quietly I rose from the bed, dressed hastily, put on the jacket you see me wearing now, kissed Rachel on the forehead, walked out of the room, and closed the door softly behind me. That was three years ago.'

Amos began to recede into himself again. His demeanour of weary indifference had returned. Pulling up the collar of his tattered coat, he stood up unsteadily and pushed his chair back. The porter Rodriguez leered at us from across the room, then winked suggestively in the direction of Lilith. Amos responded with a contemptuous snort. 'Goodnight, Henokh,' he said, 'and thanks for listening.' He trundled out of the hotel lounge, swaying a little, and vanished into the foggy crevices of the night.

Yah, said my uncle Henokh. He gazed into the bowl of his pipe, but the glow had long been extinguished. The fire in the hearth had died down as well, survived only by a dim glimmer. He relit his pipe and let fly a fresh cloud of dense, grey, aromatic smoke.

Yah, said my uncle Henokh again, the story doesn't quite end there. A few years ago I picked up a book in a downtown store, a new novel by an unknown writer. I never bought the book, but the title and author intrigued me. On the back was a photograph of the author, a rather handsome woman in her mid-forties. The novel was called *My Lost Love*. The author's name was Rachel Butterfly.

UNCLE HENOKH'S DREAM

My uncle Henokh, who at the age of eighty-five arrived at the great poker table in heaven, was not only an expert card-player but an erudite, world-travelled man. He had a neatly trimmed ginger beard, and his eyes were two blue skies of laughing sadness. He always wore black, usually in the form of a polo-neck sweater. Although my uncle Henokh was profoundly in love with God, he harboured an inborn dislike of religion and its clerics. Most of them, he maintained, had subdivided God into profitable parcels of real estate – the clergy were God's public enemy number one.

Uncle Henokh's love of storytelling was legendary. I remember him saying, 'Life on earth is a story, a story in which every living thing has its place.' To understand one's place on earth was to understand God's difficult position in heaven. But most people were *dis*placed, he explained, or they displaced themselves; they could barely find their way around their own home.

I was fifteen years old and my infatuation with my uncle Henokh knew no bounds. I wanted only to be like him, everything he said made so much sense to me. I cannot remember him ever talking out of turn – every word he spoke was apt and measured. Being a compulsive reader, my uncle was forever quoting books, ideas, thoughts. Many of the thoughts were his own, but out of modesty he always ascribed them to someone else. Once, a local loudmouth who fancied himself a scribbler tried to needle him. 'Hey, Henokh,' he said. 'You're always quoting from old books, old poets. Well, my grandfather the baker taught me that a freshly-baked bagel is much tastier than a reheated one!' 'That's very true,' my uncle shot back, 'and there is plenty of room in my heart for a baker who is a poet. But no room at all for a poet who is a baker.'

Uncle Henokh firmly believed that mankind was divided into two camps: storytellers and fools. A child who could tell a story he called a master; an adult who could not, just a boy. I can still recall with pleasure how artfully he entwined his stories with biblical resonances, and how he imbued them with his quite often daring interpretations. Sometimes this got him into hot water with his ultra-religious stepbrother, the cantor Aron. Aron claimed that Henokh was deliberately misquoting the Bible to upset him, but I secretly suspected that Aron was jealous. He envied his stepbrother's erudition, his skill at storytelling, his sonorous voice, his popularity; and above all, he resented his own wife's soft spot for her charismatic brother-in-law, whom she was always trying unsuccessfully to seduce. She came from a long line of Portuguese kabbalists and loved to talk in riddles. But even I was sometimes embarrassed by her innuendoes, and I couldn't help noticing how longingly she gazed at my uncle or the way she accidentally brushed her bosom against his ear whenever she served him at table.

Late one afternoon, as the sun was about to abandon the horizon and its last golden rays slanted through the red-embroidered edges of the clouds, my uncle Henokh, sitting in the dining-room of Aron's house amid a company of local admirers, including myself, tapped his pipe against his heel, looked around, and said: '*Yah*, gentlemen, I still can't grasp the meaning of God's testing of

Abraham. What a dark tale, what an unbelievable chapter. God is asking Abraham to kill his one and only son! And yet Isaac is the future of the Jewish people! No, I cannot accept that.'

Aron, of course, reacted at once. 'Watch out, Henokh,' he warned. 'You're questioning the Torah. Be careful, man, you're playing with fire!'

My uncle paused for a moment, lit his pipe, and then shook his head. 'Questioning, my dear Aron, is fundamental to our teachings,' he replied. 'Without questioning, there is no Bible, no Torah.'

'No Bible? No Torah? Henokh, you're a pagan, a blasphemer.' Aron's voice was steady but charged with indignation. 'You're an arrogant rogue, and you'll burn in hell.'

Henokh was unruffled by this attack. 'Aron,' he said, 'do you know why the words, *And He saw that this was good*, are specifically omitted – for the first time – after God has completed the sixth day of His labour?'

'Yes, yes, you villain, of course I know!' Aron in his agitated mood was ready to accept any challenge. 'Would you expect a God who is so fond of humility to rejoice in His own image?'

Uncle Henokh grinned. 'Aron, you may have a point there. But my guess is that the Master of the Universe, who of course lives forever, could already envisage the millions of little Arons that would emerge through the ages from the belly of His first creation.'

'My God, did the same womb give birth to me and to this creature?' cried Aron. 'Clearly, in your heart you are not circumcised. Even the Messiah will turn away from you.'

'What Messiah?' Henokh asked with mock-innocence. I was enjoying this.

'So, you don't believe in the coming of our Redeemer!' Aron was by now utterly incensed.

'No, Aron,' Henokh countered with a smile (my uncle's smile could stop a wild beast in its tracks). 'What I believe is that it is for *us* to go to *him*.'

'And how do you propose to do that?'

'Ask Isaiah, he knows.' Quietly, in his customary manner, Henokh stood up, took a few deep puffs from his pipe, and, after pacing around for a minute with his hands clasped behind his back, looked directly at Aron and added, in an almost Talmudic chant, '*Yah*, my friends, religious fanaticism is blind. Like nature, it builds by destroying.'

This was just too much for his wretched stepbrother. 'Henokh, I'm warning you. One more word, and...'

'And what, Aron? Were you about to tell me that you might be transformed into a Cain?' I was thrilled at this sinister new turn the exchange had taken. 'That would be marvellously biblical – think of it, Aron. Cain had essentially no conflict with his brother, it was a blatant case of jealousy, caused by the Almighty, so why on earth did Cain murder Abel? Do you know why, Aron? Because the Almighty was out of reach.'

Aron had risen as well, and was standing there with a contemptuous sneer on his face. 'You see, Aron,' Henokh continued, 'when a man kills another, he virtually kills God. And you would not want to do that, brother, not even for the sake of religion. Or would you?'

'Henokh, I think you'd better hold your tongue!' Aron was straining hard to maintain his composure, but it was plain that he was seething, coiled up now as tight as a spring ready to snap. 'You're on very dangerous ground, skating on very thin ice. I repeat, you'll burn in hell.'

'Well, it won't be the first time,' said my uncle Henokh. And then he produced another of his melting smiles. 'But why must we argue, Aron?' he said. 'Perhaps we are both taking ourselves too seriously. Perhaps, like the people of Shinar, although we speak the same language, we yet lack a spiritual Esperanto. Maybe it's time for mending fences,' said my suddenly conciliatory uncle Henokh. He looked around. Everyone knew what to expect next. Even Aron resumed his seat with a pious shake of the head. He reckoned that he had held his ground admirably, had even elicited a small concession from his rival.

'And the best remedy,' Henokh went on, glancing at each member of the group in turn, 'the best way to make up, is to share a story. It is written that God wanted the Jews to tell stories. To tell them, naturally, to Him.' And my uncle began to relate another of his famous tales.

Yah, last night I went to bed earlier than usual, I don't know why, but something told me, *Henokh, you are expected*. So I rushed through the evening prayer, hopped into bed and closed my eyes. Suddenly I was approached by a barefooted stranger dressed in a grey robe fastened above his loins with a string. He carried a long brown knotted cane, and he addressed me by my name.

'Hey, Henokh,' he said, 'where are you off to?'

'I don't know, sir,' I replied.

'*But I do*,' said the stranger in the grey robe. 'Look over there, into this barrel of still water. It was once a flame on a holy altar.'

I looked to where he was pointing, and as I looked the water in the barrel swirled about, like a flame in the wind, and a moment later I was able to make out a flock of birds – no, of people. *Flying* people! Something made me spread my arms out, birdlike, and before I knew it I was with them, flying through the air. I flew with them for what seemed like an hour, and then, all at once, they vanished and I was all alone – in mid-air! I looked down, but below me, for as far as I could see, there was nothing but water. I was certain I had flown into Noah's time.

Yah, you have no idea, Aron, how pleased I was to see the stranger again. 'Sir, please help me,' I implored him, 'for I am lost.'

'You are not lost, dreamer,' he answered, and, pointing with his long cane towards a spark of light, added: 'Fly to the east.'

So I flew, and flew, until I noticed the river Pishon below me, and then the Tree of Life, and I knew I was back where we had all come from. I arrived at the Garden of Eden just before the holy Sabbath, arrived to the sway of silver birches in white prayer-shawls, and a choir of candles welcoming Queen Shabbat. Aron, I was so overwhelmed I was barely able to breathe.

But I realised that I was starving. On tiptoe I approached a door that had suddenly appeared. I knocked softly, and the word *Welcome* drifted out to me through the door, which was opening slowly, like a blessing. A moment later a figure stood before me – I knew it was our Father, Abraham, looking as if he had just walked out from the pages of Genesis. We all know how the Bible lauds his hospitality. Well, within the blink of an eye he was carrying me, in his very arms, towards a table. I sat down awkwardly, and whom do you think I discovered next to me? You, Aron!

Yah, I remember how amazed I was at the way Abraham made *kiddush* – what a voice, what a melody. And yet, Aron, to be completely truthful, I must admit I detected a slight faltering note, a hint of sadness in his prayer. Perhaps it was the old man's broken heart, I thought, crying out after his young lost Hagar.

Next morning, what a sense of absolute serenity, what a holy silence! No rustle of trees, no babble of rivers, no gossip of flowers. The very angels that moved soundlessly through the air from time to time were voiceless. But if I pressed my ear to the enveloping silence, I could just distinguish, as if from a faraway world, the muffled voice of the great river Sambatyon, and it seemed to be murmuring: *Shabbat Shalom, Shabbat Shalom, Shabbat Shalom . . .*

And all at once I noticed, on your head, Aron, a halo of awe. At that moment I remember hoping that you might have grasped the biblical significance of Eve's dialogue with the snake, and of Adam's urge to self-destruction when he reached out for the secret of eternal life. But your chief observation – forgive me, Aron, it was just a dream – seemed to concern Sarah not wearing a wig, and the males not wearing *kippot*. And when you remarked upon the absence of a ritual bath, I couldn't help noticing, too, how critically you scanned the glistening naked breasts of a group of lovely angels frolicking in the water.

One morning, as we were strolling about the Orchard of Wisdom, a little white cloud accosted us. *You must be tourists*, it seemed to say. *Perhaps you would like me to show you around. There are some places of great interest, not exactly here but just nearby.*

Why not, we decided, so we followed the little cloud.

Yah, only those who have ever been to paradise are aware that hell and paradise are two faces of the same coin. One wrong step, or one right one, will get you there in the blink of an eye. All of a sudden, we – you, stepbrother, and I, and of course the little cloud – found ourselves before a gate bearing a mysterious inscription:

> *WHAT HAS BEEN WILL FOREVER BE*
> *DEATH WILL NEVER SET YOU FREE*

'What does it mean?' I asked. 'What lies beyond that gate?'

The cloud darkened visibly, but refused to respond.

The three of us walked back, deep in thought – or at least, you and I walked, while the little cloud drifted alongside. The cloud was the first to speak.

You must understand, it explained, *that I am over six thousand years old, a child of the primordial chaos. I have seen all good and evil, and everything you call history. From heaven it was easy to observe life on earth.*

'But isn't everything that has happened in our cosmos preordained, part of the divine plan?'

No sooner had you, Aron, asked this question than the little cloud turned into a puff of black smoke. As it floated away, my head was sprinkled with smouldering ash.

You know, Aron, the journey from thoughts to words can be quite arduous. But let me try to describe to you what took place afterwards. When we returned to paradise, Abraham immediately ushered us into a great hall. All the biblical luminaries were assembled around a grand mahogany table, which King Solomon himself had brought from his palace. In the centre of the table lay an open Bible, and each sage, seer, prince and scholar had to read his own page in turn. When it came to Ezekiel, the great prophet stood up and, like a turbulent flame, addressing the invisible Omnipotence, cried out: *If only You had stopped them grinding up their bones!*

Yah, a white frost descended on the holy assembly. Ezekiel's voice died away, the flame dwindled to a glimmer. To help smooth things over, the angels began to serve the banquet that had obviously been made ready. The mood changed, there was chatter, even laughter, we all relaxed a little. I was completely unprepared for what happened next.

Don't look so alarmed, Aron, it was only a dream. But even then, *you* had to have the last word. As one of the beautiful angels placed before you a bowl of the most golden chicken soup, you rose uncertainly and in your brazen voice called out, 'Is this soup kosher? Who supervised?'

The entire hall fell silent. The angel blushed, averted her eye, and pointed upwards. As for you, Aron – you looked around doubtfully, pushed the soup away, and declared: 'Maybe I'll just have an apple. But please, on a paper plate.'

Daybreak. The greyish light held its breath against the window-pane. In the dining-room of Aron's house the two stepbrothers sat facing each other across the table. They looked as if they had just returned from a long and tedious pilgrimage. Several others who had stayed through the night to listen to my uncle Henokh's story were slumped in chairs around the table.

Aron's wife walked softly into the room, rubbing her eyes. 'It's time for morning prayer,' she reminded the company. 'Breakfast will be served soon.' And almost as an afterthought she whispered: 'No bread, no Torah.'

She smiled ever so faintly in Henokh's direction, and then withdrew.

Overcome by weariness at last, and perhaps also by a desire for peace, my uncle Henokh yawned, ran his hand through his thinning hair, and nodded silently to himself. Aron, locked up in his own silence, stared out the window at the gathering day.

EMBERS

THE ETERNAL QUESTION

A young disciple was questioning his teacher. 'What should one do, rabbi,' he asked, 'to become a righteous man?'

'You might as well ask me what one should do to become king of England,' replied the rabbi.

The young man was perplexed. 'Do you mean there is no answer to my question?'

'Sit down, son,' said the other, 'and let me tell you a story. When the wisdom, generosity and foresight of Joseph, son of our patriarch Jacob, became known to the world – how he saved Egypt, how he not only forgave his brothers for selling him into slavery but restored their lives by opening Pharaoh's heart to them – when these and Joseph's many other noble deeds became known, most of mankind longed to learn from his example.'

The rabbi took a sip of his tea. 'There was a farming community that dwelt in the south of Egypt, at the very border of present-day Sudan, and they were no exception. They decided to question Joseph in person, so they set out on a journey across the hot desert, where danger lay in wait at every step. You must remember, son, that this was a time before planes, trains and cars; people had to walk or ride camels.

'They arrived in the middle of a torrid summer's day, tired, haggard, their feet bleeding and swollen. As soon as Joseph learnt of their presence, he invited them to his home, where, like his great-grandfather Abraham, he washed their bruised feet. After they had feasted on wheaten bread, goat's cheese, grapes and fresh springwater, Joseph said: "Friends, what has prompted you to come here? What compelled you to undertake this dangerous journey?" The eldest among them spoke up. "Well, sir," he began, "we came to learn from you. To discover what one should do to become righteous."

'Joseph was taken aback and for a good while stood there motionless, and silent as a man without a tongue. His guests' hearts nearly caved in out of fear. At last he smiled. "I do not know what one should do to become righteous," he said.

'The visitors broke into a soul-wrenching lament. "O great one," they cried out through their tears, "do you mean to tell us that we are to walk back to our homes with nothing?"

'Joseph shook his head. "No," he replied, "that is not what I have told you. I said that I do not know what one should do to become righteous. I do know, however, that one may become righteous by knowing precisely what one should *not* do."'

HUMILITY

There is a school of thought which upholds the idea that, simultaneously with light, God created humility. After all, He chose the Hebrew language to write the Torah because the Hebrew alphabet has no capital letters. Clearly, our Master had foreseen that capital letters would only add unnecessary aggrandisement to the many names destined to play a part in the forthcoming drama of life – not excluding, of course, His very own name as well.

A second manifestation of the premium God placed on humility was the creation of a man in His own image, but out of dust – an indisputable reminder that we should be forever mindful of what we all ultimately are.

These and related questions had come up at a conference of the letters of the Hebrew alphabet, held on cloud nine, in seventh heaven. All twenty-two letters sat in a circle. Each of them was a gateway, a tale on its own, its purpose in harmony with its form; yet any one letter without any other was but empty pride, as useful as a single link from a broken chain.

As the golden cup of joy was handed from letter to letter, and the intoxicating fluid seeped through their bones, the letters became a little conceited, each in accordance with its particular shape. The last letter of the alphabet, the Tav, which stands for Torah and for sobriety, grew quite uneasy. Awareness that such a state might compromise the modesty of his company prompted

Tav to assume, quickly but respectfully, the blue ethereal pulpit, from where he began to recount, in a sweet Talmudic chant, the following true story:

'I am sure we all remember how we were floating aimlessly around Sinai when Moses, enveloped in his mantle of blinding effulgence, came down from the mountain with his two stone tablets... And the ugly scene he confronted on his return to the valley, which provoked him to smash the tablets, along with the ten commandments engraved upon them, to grit.

'What many of you don't know is that, late at night, when the Israelites were fast asleep, God recalled the heartbroken Moses up to the mount, where, with His finger, He once more inscribed the ten commandments – but this time on tablets of the purest gold. Then the Lord spoke again to His servant, our teacher Moses, and instructed him to keep for himself all the gold that had fallen aside during the writing of the commandments.

'The angels were taken aback. Why? they wanted to know. What did this mean? What need did Moses have of all that gold?

'The Almighty smiled at His retainers: "I want Moses to be a shining example of humility," He replied. "And where is the art in a pauper being humble?"'

TO ENTER EDEN

A legend tells us that once, while on his way home from Africa, Alexander of Macedon pitched his tent near a silent lake where, at nightfall, a nymph sang him lullabies of things to come.

Alexander, she whispered, and her words overflowed with a tantalising warmth. *You have conquered most of the known world, but there is yet a land, a wonderful, wise land, which you ought to see.* 'Where is this wonderful land?' Alexander asked. *It lies to the east of our dreams.* 'And how will I get there?' the king persisted, aroused. *Follow my voice*, said the nymph, and vanished.

At daybreak Alexander set out on his journey. After walking for seven days and seven hours, he reached the first frontier. What a strange river, he thought, and how curiously divided into four branches.

Suddenly he heard the voice of the nymph once more. *The first is the Pishon, the second the Gihon, the third the Tigris, and the fourth the Euphrates.* The voice paused, then continued: *Now, my friend, if you are eventually admitted, beware of the cherubim and their fiery, ever-turning swords. And above all, do not touch the Tree, or you will suffer Adam's fate.*

And so it was that Alexander of Macedon, whose visage carried the tale of an undefeated king, stood finally and resolutely at the gates of Eden. He knocked three times.

Who is there? a voice within responded.

'Open up,' he replied. 'I am Alexander the Great, the king who has conquered the entire world.'

Sir, came the answer, *this gate is not for warriors, but only for sages.*

'Friend,' Alexander declared, 'I have journeyed at least thrice through the books of the wisest of the Greeks. What more could you require?'

We know that, Alexander, we know. Yet we still cannot let you in. Come back later – much, much later.

Alexander was bewildered. 'How late?' he asked.

After the books of wisdom have journeyed at least thrice through you.

RESTITUTION

In the fourth century before the common era, the Egyptians lodged the following complaint before Alexander the Great: 'At the time of the Exodus, the Israelites, on the advice of their leader and teacher, Moses, borrowed from us various objects of silver and gold and many items of sumptuous clothing, and took these with them into the desert. In the name of justice, we demand that this property be returned to us, the heirs of its rightful and legitimate owners.'

The Israelites were taken aback. The case seemed clear-cut. How were they going to defend it? As they pondered their predicament, a hunchback by the name of Gviah ben Koosm came to them and offered his services. He was well-known among the locals for his crafty ways and agile mind, so the Israelites accepted his offer.

The court was duly convened. The young king gazed down upon ben Koosm and wondered what manner of argument such a puny, deformed individual could advance against a claim that appeared so strong. The Egyptians restated their case, and then the hunchback was ordered to respond.

'From where,' he asked the plaintiffs' spokesman with great deliberation, 'did you derive the idea that you have the right to make such an outlandish demand?'

'Why, from your very own Torah,' the other shot back with a triumphant gleam in his eye.

'Very well, I too will present evidence from our Torah,' ben Koosm replied, 'and then we shall let our good king decide whose case has more merit.' He bowed his head towards Alexander and approached the throne. 'Sire,' he began, 'my people were initially invited to sojourn as free settlers in Egypt. But then an evil pharaoh turned us into slaves. He commanded that all our baby boys be murdered, he appointed ruthless taskmasters over us, and he made us perform inhuman labours beneath their vicious whips. We toiled in misery, deprived of food and water, naked and wretched and racked with pain under the scorching rays of the sun. Our days and nights were without hope, and our wages were death.

'Your majesty, we dwelt in Egypt for 432 years. I have calculated that one year of work under the conditions I have described is equivalent to at least ten years of a normal labouring life. Therefore, great ruler, our counterclaim is as follows: The Egyptians owe the Israelites payment for 4300 years of labour. Let them pay us what they owe us, and my people will immediately restore to them all the objects and items they accuse us of having stolen.'

A hubbub of anxious, confused chatter arose from among the Egyptians like a hot desert wind in a hollow chimney. And when the king lifted his head to pronounce judgment, he was startled to observe that all the plaintiffs had vanished. The chamber's doors stood wide open, like a great mouth whose speech has been stifled and stilled.

THE TEST

Ptolemy, ruler of Egypt, military successor to Alexander of Macedon, was a powerful and intelligent monarch. However, he found the Jewish notion of one God quite bizarre. 'Look,' he argued, 'if I myself, with the assistance of all my gods, am hard-pressed to rule Egypt, how can a single god rule over the whole wide world?' No, it was impossible, he concluded, the Jews must be lying – they must have more than one god. And he, Ptolemy, would unmask their trickery.

So one bright morning, as the sun-king stirred the day to life, he crawled out from under his sumptuous silky bedding, downed two large goblets of strong wine (woe to a people whose ruler drinks in the morning!), and then, purring like an expectant lion, sat down to a huge breakfast banquet.

Fed and sated, he entered the palace temple, where he consulted his panoply of gods in the matter of how to deal with the Jews, whose father Abraham had dared not only to smash the old gods of Terah but had heralded the presence of an *invisible* yet *living* Almighty – one whose existence was claimed to over-reach that of all other gods.

'Let us prove them wrong!' said Ptolemy to his leading clay god, reputed to be an offspring of the formidable Osiris. 'We will assemble seventy-two Jewish sages, and usher them into seventy-two locked cubicles – not telling them, of course, what we have in mind. Once they are securely locked in, these Jews will be ordered to rewrite their Torah – but only in Greek, so that we might all be able to understand. And so help us, Ra, we'll quickly catch them out.'

As soon as the six dozen sages were locked into their cubicles and ordered to rewrite the Torah, they caught on to Ptolemy's wicked intention. They implored heaven to have mercy upon them, and begged God to enable them to think and respond as one. Then they started to write.

But a strange and marvellous thing happened. When they picked up their pens to inscribe the opening lines of the Bible, they did not write, as it is written, 'In the beginning God created the heaven and the earth.' To a man they wrote instead, 'God, in the beginning, created the heaven and the earth.' For they somehow knew what Ptolemy would have said: If the beginning came before God, then the beginning must also be a god!

A little later they wrote, each in concert with the others, how God had stated, 'I shall make a man in my own image' – rather than, as it is written, 'Let us make a man in our own image.' Again, they knew that Ptolemy would have said: If your god is indeed a single god, why talk of 'we' and 'our', rather than 'I' and 'my'?

And so it went.

After many weeks, their task accomplished, the sages emerged. As they filed out of the hall they were smiling serenely, and each was bathed in a halo of dazzling radiance. Ptolemy found himself speechless, and had to shield his eyes.

A HISTORICAL DILEMMA

It is said that Ben-Sira was born a sage, and that he began to speak when still at his mother's breast. At the age of one he was already studying with a rabbi; at seven he knew all the secrets of the holy Torah.

The mighty king of Babylon, Nebuchadnezzar, admired but at the same time despised Ben-Sira. In public he would proclaim, 'Ben-Sira is my good friend,' but in his heart he harboured jealousy and hatred, to the point of murder.

So one day, in a moment of great spiritual exaltation, when it seemed to him that there was nothing in the world more splendid and fascinating than he himself, Nebuchadnezzar summoned Ben-Sira and demanded his advice.

'Ben-Sira,' he declared, 'if you can find a solution to my dilemma, I'll reward you with the right to break bread at my table. There is a man whom I hate,' he went on, 'yet we speak as friends. Would it be wise to poison his food, so that he may die?'

'O great king,' answered the sage, 'permit me to tell you a parable which may throw a light into the darkness that dwells within your question.'

Nebuchadnezzar nodded and listened.

'The mighty king Nimrod,' Ben-Sira began, 'possessed a magnificent horse – a horse whose beauty knew no bounds. All the other horses in the kingdom were jealous, and plotted against Nimrod's cherished steed. They sent a delegation. "If you permit us to chop off your head," they said to the handsome animal, "we will reward you with a stable full of hay and barley."

'But Nimrod's horse, who was not only beautiful but clever, immediately saw through their design. "Fools," he replied. "If you chop off my head, who is going to eat the hay and barley?"

'And so, glorious ruler,' Ben-Sira concluded, 'if you poison me, how will I be able to break bread at your table?'

THE CONTENTIONS OF THE TREES

In the time of antiquity, the mooncalf king Ahasuerus reigned over a kingdom that stretched form India to Ethiopia. His trusted minister, Haman, son of Hammedatha the Agagite, was descended from the lowest ranks of society. It was said that he had once run a bathhouse where people were disburdened of their lice. Yet this Haman had grand ambitions, and dreams that gave him sleepless nights. Lying next to his ugly wife Zeresh, he coveted the beautiful Jewish queen, Esther; and he coveted the monarch's crown.

But how could a man of such low breeding achieve these things? Only by means of intrigue, deceit, and murder. The Jews, who refused to bow down before Haman, became his bane and his obsession – an obsession that eventually destroyed him. For what this rascal omitted from his calculations was Esther's love for her own people, and the wisdom of her uncle Mordechai – who cleverly turned the tables on the schemer, so that Ahasuerus swiftly learnt of Haman's intentions. The king ordered the offender to be hanged from a fifty-cubit tree.

'I'm in a lucky position,' said the grapevine. 'Not only am I too small for the job, but one should not forget it was I who provided the first offering for the holy altar.'

'And who furnished the Menorah with oil?' replied the olive tree. 'I'm out of the question.'

'And everyone knows,' asserted the date tree, 'that the Psalms equate me with goodness. So how could I be charged with such a wretched duty?'

'And remember, it is with my fruit that the Jews praise the Creator,' declared the citron tree. 'You can certainly count me out.'

'And I held a special status in the Garden of Eden,' proclaimed the apple tree. 'For me to undertake such a thing would be absurd.'

Then the fig tree, the myrtle and the cedar all had their say, and each of them argued convincingly against being used as the gallows for Haman.

Finally the thorn tree spoke. 'Please, good trees, listen to me. My life has no meaning, I don't serve any purpose. Look at me – all dryness and spikes. Let me, for once, be of service to humanity.'

The other trees listened and were moved. They agreed that there was no other way, so the task was given to the thorn tree.

But when Haman felt the noose tighten around his neck, the thorn tree began to weep.

'Why are you crying?' the condemned man asked. 'After all, you volunteered.'

'Yes,' said the thorn tree. 'But I would never have believed, in all my rotten life, that even I could fall so low, so very low.'

THE WISDOM CHAIR

Nebuchadnezzar, the cruel ruler of Babylon, pictured himself as a god and dreamt of conquering posterity. What caused him sleepless nights, however, was King Solomon's golden Wisdom Chair. It was not that he doubted his own superior sagacity, for no dunce ever does; but he had been told by his royal seers that the possession of Solomon's chair would ensconce him in perpetuity amid the loftiest echelons of history and lore.

According to legend, the Wisdom Chair was made of gold flown in by a flock of angels from Havila, land of the Garden of Eden. Bezalel, a descendant of the very Bezalel who had constructed the Tabernacle and the three lidless arks, led the team of craftsmen, who mixed gold with Solomon's wisdom. The stepped pathway that led up to the chair was guarded by twelve gold lions and twelve gold eagles – lion facing eagle, eagle facing lion, each pair at a higher level than the last.

Nebuchadnezzar was delighted with the plunder brought back by his generals after the destruction of the holy temple in Jerusalem, but the most coveted prize of all was Solomon's chair. The excitement of having it in his possession made the king pleasantly drowsy. He needed to rest, so he reclined on one of the hanging beds in the opulent gardens of his palace. Presently he was startled by the sound of footsteps. He raised himself up and saw – an apparition.

'Nebuchadnezzar,' it addressed him. 'Like most of your kind, you shall be cloned and recloned, again and again. But do not dare to desecrate King Solomon's chair.'

'Kill him! Kill him!' the king screamed.

'Kill whom, noble sovereign?' asked the astonished seers standing nearby. They could see no intruder.

'Oh... I had a dream, an awful vision,' said the king, his face darkening.

'Tell us, noble sovereign, tell us,' the leading seer urged him. 'There is nothing in the world that can be hidden from me.'

So Nebuchadnezzar described what he had seen and heard.

The leading seer reflected for a moment. 'Well, my lord,' he announced at last. '*Clone* is assuredly a word from a future world. In your case, it simply means you will live forever. As for desecrating the chair – pay no heed to it, sire. It is clearly a provocation from the magicians of the Hebrews.'

With racing pulse and radiant visage, Nebuchadnezzar approached the Wisdom Chair. To the general applause of the assembled seers, he ascended the steps leading up to the chair, one by one. But as he was about to claim the twelfth and highest level, the uppermost golden lion lifted up its mighty paw and, with one great swipe, hurled the king who would be god down from his great height and into the abyss of eternal infamy.

THE RIGHTEOUS

An old legend tells of how, in the time of our first destruction, as the Babylonians were plundering the holy temple and carrying off its treasures, the prophet Jeremiah darted among the toppling, smoke-enveloped walls and deftly tore out, by its roots, the eternal flame of human decency that burned on the holy altar, then carefully hid it in a cave on Mount Nabu. The flame, by its own wisdom, transformed itself into an ice-cold lake.

Seventy years later, when the Jews returned from their Babylonian captivity and restored the temple to its former glory, they were horrified when the dry twigs and other tinder they placed on the altar refused to ignite. Luckily there was an old man who remembered what Jeremiah had done. He went to the cave, found the lake, and no sooner had he poured a bucket of its ice-cold water on the reluctant twigs, than the flame leapt into life and began to sing a song of joyous rebirth.

But what happened to the flame after the second destruction, following the legendary Bar-Kochba's defeat? No one knows.

This was the very question I was pondering one morning on my travels, years ago. As the silvery mist rose over the nearby hills, as the first cock crowed the world back to life, I entered a still-drowsing village inn where I encountered an elderly stranger. His name was Ariel. He was obviously a seer, probably a kabbalist, because without asking me what I wanted he winked me over and invited me to dig into his pot of steaming porridge.

I thanked him and accepted his offer, for I was very hungry. While we shared the meal, I noticed that he was mumbling under his breath. At first his words made no sense; but gradually, as I listened more closely, I was able to follow what he was saying.

'You want to know... you want to know...' he kept repeating. 'You want to know the unknown.'

Puzzled by his meaning but greatly intrigued, I felt compelled to nod in agreement. Almost at once his mutterings changed into an eerie, half-melodic recitation.

'After the second destruction,' he chanted, 'and also after the third, there were no prophets, no prophets. So the flame, like its people, went into exile. And there, in the midst of the most heinous crimes, the flame of human decency transformed itself, by its own wisdom, into millions of tiny sparks – sparks of hope – which the exiles warmed in their bosoms for thousands of years. And it is said,' he continued, 'that during the time of despair, some of the sparks found their way into the hearts of certain people who were not exiles.'

He paused, and for the first time pierced me with his gaze. 'These we called the Righteous,' he said.

A DEADLY MISTAKE

Joshua, a noble and elderly kabbalist, lived with his one and only disciple, Akiba, in a white cottage under a pitched red roof somewhere in a township in the mountains. Every morning they swam in the crisp waters of a nearby lake. After a frugal breakfast they would embark on a long walk, and the kabbalist would commence the daily instruction of his disciple. He talked about the meaning of life and death, and the need to be at peace with oneself.

One day in early spring, as the first rays of light slanted through the torn morning clouds, Joshua called his student to his bedside. Opening his deep brown eyes, like a peregrine who craves to clench his mind around the picture of his little home before embarking on a journey from which he knows not when he will return, the kabbalist addressed his companion.

'Akiba, my son,' he said. 'I am about to go the way of my fathers. Please see to it that I receive a decent burial.'

By midday the old scholar was no more. Akiba took his master's corpse to the mortuary, where he was informed that the funeral would take place on the morrow.

The following day Akiba arrived well before the appointed hour, for he wanted to look upon the face of his beloved teacher one last time. There were two coffins standing side by side, and when he opened the one marked *Joshua*, the young man almost fainted. It held the body of Zanvel the street-sweeper, who had always borne a resemblance to the old kabbalist.

'Gentlemen!' he cried. 'Gentlemen, please, you are making a horrible mistake.' But no one would listen to him – the coffins, after all, were clearly marked. When they reached the graveyard, the kabbalist was thrown into a rough pit and buried without a word. The street-sweeper was interred with all the pomp and dignity befitting a respected elder.

That night the kabbalist visited Akiba in a dream. 'Why, rabbi?' the young disciple pleaded. 'Tell me why!'

His teacher seemed to smile. 'You see, my dear Akiba,' he said, 'heaven records everything, and dishes out rewards and punishments accordingly. Once, as a member of a circle of learned colleagues, I witnessed how a friend was accused of a crime he had never committed, yet I did not stand up in his defence.

'But Zanvel the simpleton, on one of his daily rounds years ago, spotted a stray dog whose front paws were broken. It was whimpering in the gutter, many people were passing but no one took notice of its agony. Zanvel carried the dog home and nursed it back to health.'

'What happened then?' Akiba asked.

'Nothing. The dog lived out its days with Zanvel.'

THE PROMISE

It happened around the time of Passover. Unexpectedly, the days in heaven grew hotter. On their way home from synagogue Abraham and Sarah stopped at the local swimming-pool just to soak their feet, swollen from the long walk. They sat and chatted on the pool's edge.

'You know, Abraham, the weather of late has become terribly unseasonable. Isn't it time, my husband, to have a word or two with our MC about the climate?'

'No, my dear Sarah, it has nothing to do with Him, not any more. Your forget that control of the weather was handed over to the department of political affairs.'

'Well, this time last year you promised that our place of prayer next door would be ready for *Yontov*, and yet you still haven't even started to pour the foundations.'

'It's not my fault, dear, it's the council. Not only are they tangled up in hundreds of different regulations, which they keep amending from day to day to make our life difficult, but some-one is pulling strings against us behind the scenes.'

'Haven't you got any friends on that council?'

'Sure. And friends are great. The trouble is, they can never be counted upon when you need them. At the last meeting everything was nearly settled, but then, out of the blue, my brother, my very own brother Haran, raised an objection.'

'An objection? On what grounds?'

'He claimed our synagogue will be too close to his; and that our prayer will therefore interfere with his prayer.'

'Typical, just typical. Exactly like down there. Obviously they're aping us – or is it the other way round? Can't you *do* something?'

'You know, Sarah, I'm hungry, and a nagging wife is like a dripping tap.'

'Fine, but don't expect me to hold my tongue.'

'Never!'

'And what's more, we're not eating tonight until you answer a simple question. Tell me, my husband, will our people ever be united?'

'We *are* united, Sarah, in a way.'

'I can't see it. If brother and brother in heaven are at logger-heads, how can the promised land unite our children?'

'The land cannot and will not. But the Promise will, and does. And don't forget, it was His idea?'

'I think He's a little like you. Promises, always promises...'

THE RING

Early one Friday morning, Isaac ben Abraham went down to the Jerusalem market, where he bought from Ishmael ben Abraham, for one piastre, an oversized silvery fish. Delighted, Isaac carried the bargain home and presented it to his wife Rebecca, so that she might cook his catch for their Sabbath meal.

Isaac was a profoundly pious man, of a fine and poetic disposition. As he walked slowly home from the synagogue that evening, he attuned his delicate ear to the melodious effulgence of the stars and, in concert with the whole universe, sang the traditional welcome to the incoming Queen Sabbath.

Stepping over the threshold of his home, he was greeted by his children, and by an excited smile from his lovely Rebecca. 'You know, my husband,' she said, barely able to contain herself, 'while preparing your fish, I found in its belly a beautiful golden ring set with three gorgeous rubies. Doubtless it once adorned the finger of a sultan's daughter – it must be worth a mountain of gold. I don't think, Isaac, that you'll ever need to work again. From now on you can spend your days studying your beloved Torah.'

'No, my wife,' Isaac replied at once. 'Firstly, to pay with such money for studying our holy scriptures would be to tarnish every letter of their sacred text. Secondly, Rebecca, your husband bought only the fish from Ishmael, not the ring – it belongs to him. Quite possibly he put it there himself for safekeeping and entirely forgot about it.'

And so, scarcely had the holy Sabbath made its way back to heaven than Isaac once again entered the back alleyways of Ishmael's quarter. Suddenly, out of the dark, a gang of thugs sprang upon him. After beating him mercilessly, they went through all his pockets. They found nothing. Bloodied all over, Isaac staggered to Ishmael's door. Soon he had told him the whole story. 'And where is the ring?' Ishmael enquired at last.

'In order to find the ring,' answered Isaac, 'those ruffians would have had to dissect me as my wife dissected the fish! So if you'll permit me, brother, to spend the night in your house, I promise you'll have the ring back in your hand with the first spark of light.'

YUDA THE SEER

Yuda Ben Yerukhim was an extraordinary man. Born completely blind, he was yet an avid reader; partially deaf, he was yet a fine violinist; afflicted with a stutter, he was yet a formidable debater. Yuda knew the art of blending the reticent with the acerbic, the sober with the irrational, the profound with the profane, and his words always carried a touch of irony. He claimed he could see the hues of the wind, the shapes of a storm, the colours of a melody.

But if you asked him how it was possible, he could not say. 'The words to explain it evade me, and those at hand are inadequate to translate my strange ability into language. And yet, perhaps it is fair to remark,' he would go on, 'that to see things the way I do – to perceive how the dawn makes his approach, how the silvery mist rises over the wide river, how the green forest emerges at daybreak from the white fog – for that, my friends, one needs to have the privilege of being blind, a privilege so profusely bestowed on me by our benevolent God.'

At other times Yuda would declare: 'Why me? What great service have I performed for the Master of the Universe to deserve such an honour? And yet, on balance, who am I to question the wisdom of the Almighty? Perhaps it is better, even healthier, to peer into our wretched world through unseeing eyes.'

The town's rabbi, who was not too smart, argued: 'One should never complain about one's lot because everything in life is preordained. Obviously the Master of the Universe has a firm plan to maintain on earth, and that plan must include an allotted number of the lame, the deaf, the dumb, and (above all) the blind.' Yuda would not enter into a debate with his rabbi; he would rather argue with God Himself – though he knew that in both cases it was impossible to win.

One afternoon, as Yuda sat peacefully on his porch gazing into the dark-blue marble of the shimmering horizon, reflecting on whence had come this gift of seeing things with such amazing clarity, he was suddenly reminded of a story his father had told him long ago. He could remember his father's very words:

'The Baal Shem Tov spoke of a light that existed in the days of Creation, a light which enabled one to see the whole wide world at once, from one end to the other. Then our Almighty, in His infinite wisdom, realised that such a light could pose a great danger; it might even cause a blindness greater than that which He had prescribed. So God took the light away, and hid it. And Yuda, where do you think our Master hid this special light?' His father had smiled and announced triumphantly: 'Why, in the pages of our Torah!'

'Now my son,' he had concluded, 'as you know so well, through the prism of Torah one can see the whole wide world, even if one is blind.'

THE PENALTY

The blacksmith Joel of Rava, a township in central Poland, was a man of enormous strength. It was said that he carried his hammer and anvil as another might carry a pair of pliers. No wonder a man of his might had a voracious stomach. Indeed, Joel's breakfast consisted of a hefty loaf of rye bread and two dozen fried eggs, washed down with a five-litre bucket of milk. For dinner he could consume a young ox.

His wife Pearl, who walked about the house like a frightened bird and was always dressed in black, had a decent wart on her chin and squinted cross-eyed through cloudy eyes practically devoid of brows. Yet Joel loved his wife more than anything in the world.

On Thursdays, market day, Joel never worked. Instead, from early in the morning he would position himself in a prominent spot at the marketplace to keep an eye on the local thugs, who used to taunt and sometimes physically harass the small Jewish stallkeepers. These hoodlums knew well that to mess with Joel's fists was a sure invitation to paradise.

One Friday morning a rumour seized Rava by the throat like a hangman's noose: Joel had fallen ill! It couldn't be – how could it be? I'd sooner believe, whispered one local to another, that the Sahara has been emptied of its sand. Pearl ran from doctor to doctor, from quack to seer, but no one knew what had caused the giant's indisposition. Joel lay draped across his bed like an emasculated Samson after his haircut. As a last resort, Pearl ran to fetch the rabbi.

'So tell me, Joel,' the rabbi enquired, 'tell me exactly what you did this morning, before you began to feel sick.'

The big man tried to collect his thoughts. 'Well, rabbi,' he began in a faint voice, 'when my Pearl went out to do her Friday shopping, I was eating my usual breakfast...' He stroked his beard to jog his memory. 'Ah, yes – a rooster we had bought the day before flew up, onto the table, and right into my face. I guess he was looking for crumbs.'

'What did you do?' said the rabbi.

'Why, I chased him off.'

'And then?'

'Nothing to speak of. The bird gave me a cheeky look, crowed at me loudly, and walked away. Don't you worry, you nasty little *cock-a-doodle-doo*, I called after him. You'll make a fine chicken soup!'

'Aha – mental cruelty! We must declare a fast.'

THE ESSENCE

Zev Solomon was a large, tall, broad-shouldered man. He had one brown beady eye, like that of a restless fox; the other was covered with a black patch, apparently almost since birth. His chalk-white face was encircled by a lush unkempt beard, and he walked with a limp. Because of the eyepatch and the limp, people called him 'the pirate'.

And yet, despite his alarming appearance, this wealthy merchant was a man of great compassion, a just man with a heart of gold. There was not a hospital, a school, an orphanage or a synagogue in town which had not been built, or at least endowed, with Zev Solomon's money. And everything he did was without noise or fanfare: on the quiet, so to speak. All suggestions that he should have his name attached to his benevolent enterprises he rejected with the reply, 'Why tarnish God's name on earth?'

His weekdays were crowded with activity – meetings, dealings, transactions and negotiations – but the evenings, and especially of course the Sabbath, were dedicated exclusively to the study of Talmudic erudition. Learning that led to good deeds was more important to Zev Solomon than prayer.

At thirty he had become engaged to the Rabbi's clever daughter, the blond, skinny, almost translucent Surcia. His wife-to-be was as thin and yellow as straw, and for this she had been nicknamed 'Shtrana'. Wicked tongues had it that she would not emerge alive from her first nuptial experience; yet Surcia not only gave Zev ten robust sons but – with the help of her loyal servant, the young widow Fyga – ran an excellent household whose doors were always open.

One evening, as Zev Solomon was bent in deep thought over his Talmud, and the light of the stars glinted across his inner horizon, and he pondered the harmony of God's universe, and admired the beauty and logic of His creation, there was a gentle knock on the door of his study. Zev lifted his bushy head. 'What is it, Surcia?' he asked softly. His wife slipped into the room.

'Well, husband,' she began, 'I am taking our servant Fyga to the rabbinical court.'

Zev was puzzled. 'Why? What has this hard-working creature done to you?'

Surcia shifted her negligible weight from one leg to the other. 'She has grown rather slack of late. And more importantly, I don't like the way she's been looking at our eldest son. It seems to me that she has forgotten her status as a poor widow – a widow with a child to boot.'

Zev Solomon pondered his wife's words. 'Well, now,' he replied at last, 'a widow, too, is entitled to a life, is she not? However, if you believe you have a case to present to the rabbinical court, then we must go there at once.'

'No, husband, not *we*. I wish to go on my own. I know how to present a case, and I know my rights.'

'That is very true, my dear Surcia, very true,' said Zev Solomon, 'for you are, after all, a rabbi's daughter. But you must remember,' he added with a smile, 'that your servant Fyga is not.'

TOO SMALL TO BE GREAT

No one knew from where the family Vishnicer, the richest in the town of Dremianka, had come. They lived in a timber house painted white, beneath a terracotta roof, and the blue blinds printed with little white flowers obscured their windows and kept curiosity at bay. Their chimney, however, was constantly smoking, for Chaim Vishnicer's wife, Dvosha, cooked barley soup and meat twice a week; while for breakfast all the members of the family would dip freshly-baked rolls worthy of Eden into a jar of luscious rustic honey.

The whole of Dremianka not only envied the Vishnicers, but suspected them of some manner of underhandedness. Primarily, of course, it was on account of the barley soup, the meat, and the rolls with rustic honey; but one cannot overlook the fact that Chaim Vishnicer knew how to read and write the Cyrillic alphabet, spoke to his wife and children only in Russian, and, on top of all that, was given to publishing Yiddish verses in the local newspaper. In any case, the enigma of the Vishnicers, especially that surrounding the family's wealth, gave rise to a host of rumours, which would periodically descend on the town like swarms of prickly horseflies.

According to one such rumour, Dvosha at sixteen had been a stunning beauty. In 1858 an intrepid courier of Tsar Alexander, while darting through Dremianka, had spotted her and fallen madly in love with her. When she refused his advances, the hapless fellow had presented her with a sack filled with gold, and hanged himself.

Another rumour had it that Chaim, with his flat nose and bent legs, was nothing less than a *gilgul*. In his previous life he had been a great and mighty general who had fought and single-handedly defeated a whole regiment of Tatars, and by means of his prophetic poetry had succeeded in converting them all to Judaism – for which he had been rewarded with heaps of diamonds and a harem of wives. (Obviously, since polygamy was outlawed amongst Jews, he had taken only the diamonds.)

Human beings are funny creatures. Chaim Vishnicer, who had a seat near the synagogue's eastern wall, knew that all these stories were figments of the townspeople's imaginations. Nevertheless, they eventually went to his head. He began to speak with a different tone of voice, assumed a more erect stance, affected a military, even aggressive gait. The town rabbi looked at him obliquely, and awaited the proper moment to bring Chaim to his senses.

One afternoon, on opening the latest issue of the local Jewish journal, Chaim was delighted to discover his most recent verse printed there – a little poem of which he was particularly proud. He read the lines three or four times, checked his image in the mirror, asked Dvosha for a plate of hot barley soup, and went straight to the synagogue – where he placed himself in the last seat of the back row, the paupers' section. Presently the rabbi winked him over.

'Reb Chaim,' he said, 'please go back to your seat by the eastern wall. You are not yet so great, to make yourself so small.'

SUSPICION

In the valley of dreams there had dwelt, since time immemorial, a peaceful farming community. They were simple people, comfortable and set in their ways. In spring they sowed, in summer they watched their crops grow, in autumn they harvested them, and in winter they drank hot tea, played dominoes and, out of sheer boredom, impregnated their womenfolk. Their lives, like those of all people, had their share of squabbles, sorrows and small joys.

Nothing ever altered here. If perchance a passing traveller brought news of changes in the outside world, and suggested that it was time for the community to follow suit, they would immediately expel the devious agitator and bar him from ever returning into their midst.

The community was run by a council of the ten most important farmers, and headed by a wise old chieftain who, like the other farmers, was unlearned but knew a great deal about human character and about life in general. Small wonder that under such capable leadership all conflicts were settled amicably and life remained orderly and peaceful.

But as history reminds us, nothing can last forever.

One autumn, no rains came. There was no sun in spring, the summer was dry, and the crops were miscarried by the unnourished soil. A sombre despair descended on the valley, a suspicious silence. As the next winter approached, the council of ten was secretly convened in the middle of the night and, behind drawn curtains, began to discuss the perilous situation. Unexpectedly, before five minutes had passed, the village cleric, cloaked in his black glory, entered the room.

'Gentlemen, please forgive me for appearing here uninvited,' he announced, 'but my special relationship with heaven compels me to voice my opinion on the present and very crucial moment in our history.'

'Then we will hear you,' the assembly murmured as one.

'Speak up,' said the old chieftain.

The cleric cleared his throat. 'Citizens,' he began, 'my theological experience tells me that sin is the cause of every punishment, sin is at the root of all misfortune. Sin, sin, and again, sin. I therefore propose that this venerable council should, from daybreak tomorrow, embark upon a relentless investigation of our community. Scour the streets, search all houses, rooms, alcoves, attics. We'll soon find tangible evidence to confirm our worst suspicions. Once the sinners have been rooted out and punished, our troubles will be over.'

The old chieftain scanned the blank faces of his fellow councillors. 'Very well,' he said at last. 'Let us begin the search at daybreak. And we'll start in our very own homes.'

BEDFELLOWS

Getzel the cobbler, a native of Anatevka, kept journeying the Bible in search of an answer. Why is it, he wanted to know, that evil dwells so comfortably in the bosom of a fool? And how did it so cunningly outsmart our righteous Noah?

He took off on his travels again one evening, right after work. The air was still, yet the candle in front of Getzel flickered this way and that, and the wax dripped. Before long, after a short trip through Genesis, he arrived at Chapter Seven Street, where a gold sign on a blue door read: *Noah, son of Lamech, the only righteous man of his time.*

Timorously Getzel knocked on the door, and there he stood – the white-bearded legendary Noah. 'Please enter, Getzel the cobbler from Anatevka,' said the tzaddik, 'and let me tell you how it was.' With great reverence Getzel entered the cramped dwelling.

'The earth became corrupt before God,' Noah began. 'Not as corrupt as in your time, far from it, but corrupt enough for God to decide to bring a flood that would put an end to all living flesh. The Almighty drew me aside and said, *But I will establish My covenant with you. Build an ark, and take into the ark all your household, as well as one male and one female of every animal and bird.* And He added with a heavy heart, almost pleadingly, *Please, Noah, make your work last one hundred and twenty years.* The Lord must have been hoping that somehow, from somewhere, a noble

Jonah might turn up and convince this evil world to transform itself into one great Nineveh. But His hope was in vain. Nothing could move the wild hearts of all those sinful people, nothing at all.

'In time the waters began to rise up and the ark gave a shudder. Suddenly I heard a scream. "Noah! Don't you dare leave me behind!" It was the voice of Evil, I recognised it. "Rascal," I cried, "all this is because of you!" But Evil was ready with an answer. "Noah, I was told that you are righteous. If you let me drown, you will surely be pencilled by our scribes onto a page of our holy Bible as nothing but a common murderer."

'That would indeed be a terrible result, I thought. But my God, what was I to do? My good wife came to my rescue. "You are alone," she told Evil, "and the Master's orders were strict – couples only."

'Evil ran around frantically, seeking a way out. Then it spotted the Fool sitting high in the branches of a tree. You see, Getzel, Evil may never be wise, but it is forever cunning. Within minutes, Evil had persuaded the Fool to be its bedfellow.'

BROTHERS ACROSS TIME

In the ancient city of Shushan there lived a man, a Benjaminite, known as Mordechai the Righteous. Centuries later, in the city of Warsaw, there lived another man, a well-respected Israelite, known as Korczak the Educator. Mordechai and Korczak were brothers by blood, but even more so by their love of their children, a love which was returned to them tenfold.

In that same Shushan there also resided a man called Haman, the very Haman who appears elsewhere in these narratives: Haman, son of Hammedatha, descended from Agag, king of Amalek. Centuries later, there lived a second Haman who dwelt in Warsaw and the other cities of the realm. They were blood-brothers united by a hatred for children – especially Jewish children.

And it happened that one afternoon, quite unexpectedly, the Educator's world was violently disrupted by this perfidious brother of the first Haman. The sun was completing its radiant transit of the sky, and the children of Korczak's orphanage were rehearsing *The Sick Boy*, a play by Tagore, when the younger Haman burst in.

'I have come to collect your children,' he screamed.

'We are ready,' said the Educator.

'No, not you, just them,' he corrected him.

'I am one of them,' Korczak replied, 'wherever they go, I'll go.' And he arranged his children in pairs, and placed himself at the front. And holding hands, they sang their way into the arms of Haman's laughing dead.

What of the children of Shushan? Did Mordechai's wisdom save them from their Haman? The Scriptures say that it did. Here is what happened. Mordechai had been teaching his students the meaning of the *Omer* (the sheaf of corn used as a measure of weight) when he spotted from the window the approach of his enemy. Not knowing that the villain had been ordered by King Ahasuerus to come and do honour to Mordechai, the sage cried out in alarm: 'Run, children – run for your lives, my little lambs. Run to wherever you can, save yourselves!'

As in one voice, the students shouted, 'No!' They gathered around Mordechai. 'We will not run,' they said. 'We'd rather die with prayers on our lips – but together with our beloved rabbi.'

In Warsaw, however, all those centuries later, there was no last-minute intervention from on high, no misunderstanding of Haman's intentions. Korczak the Educator and his children had nowhere to run.

RUVEN'S STORY

Born in 1922, I was the only son of Mendel and Miriam Himel. Father was a well-known lumber merchant and a learned man. People used to say that Mendel dwelt in the Talmud, and the Talmud dwelt in him. He was a good provider and we led a comfortable life. Mother was an accredited accountant; when war broke out in 1939 she was visiting her sister in New York. And I, Ruven, their fair, dark-eyed, sportive son, was a second-year student in the local high school.

Now all of that is history.

In the summer of 1944, on a Friday afternoon in the dying days of August – as a smoky sheen, like a calcium-white gauze, invaded the air over Birkenau – a group of six bewildered men, whose fate had been sealed with their birth, sat in a circle in the space between blocks 5 and 7.

'Gentlemen,' said my father. 'I have heard that our Block-führer – who likes to play William Tell with Jewish boys and laughs hoarsely when the apple survives the game unscarred – has organised a regular Kindergarten Day. He selects a hundred children aged from five to ten, feeds them with a hot thick potato soup, and teaches them to sing this German scout song:

My hat, it has three corners
Three corners has my hat
And had it not three corners
It would not be my hat.

Then he arranges the little ones in pairs, orders them to hold each other's hand, and ushers them singing into the gas chamber. . .

'Friends,' my despairing father went on, 'thousands of innocent people – men, women and children – are murdered here day after day, day after day. If God is almighty, and there is no question that He is, then surely He is guilty of murder. Therefore, He must be condemned and sentenced to death.'

Our verdict was unanimous. The sentence was proclaimed.

Resigned, almost swooning from the ordeal, my emaciated father stood up. Five pairs of eyes bored into his extinct face. Perhaps, I thought, he is already outside, beyond the boundaries of his body. And yet, a moment later, I was amazed to hear his voice come strong and resolute: 'Jews,' he said, 'the trial is over. It's time for afternoon prayer.'

Two days later, as he froze to attention during the morning selection, trying to appear strong, death pointed a finger at my forty-year-old father. As if in slowmotion, he turned his head towards me and feebly uttered: '*Shema Yisrael*, God is one.'

That night, lying awake on my lice-infested bunk while the moon hid her shameless face beneath a torn blanket of cloud, I heard a voice – the voice of a vision. *Ruven, Ruven*, the vision said, *I have served many, many gods. Your father's is the luckiest of them all.*

PAINFUL LOGIC

Simon and Ezra, two self-taught scholars, were sitting on the banks of a river one summery afternoon, discussing the Bible. Simon – impassioned, assertive, deeply religious – had all the answers; while Ezra – ironic, reticent, profoundly sceptical – had a myriad questions.

'You know, Ezra, whenever I study Genesis, I have this awesome feeling that I'm sitting in a cosmic theatre witnessing the unfolding of a mysterious drama, the drama of creation. And I am amazed by the logic of the Producer – the brilliance of His mind, the complexity of His thought, the simplicity of His language. Ezra, my friend, reading the first chapter of Genesis is a breathtaking experience, a lofty adventure akin to flying.'

'That is true, Simon, very true. Our Master certainly engineered Creation with a brilliance of mind. But in my opinion, there was no heart in it.'

'No heart! How can you say that? What about all the heartfelt miracles He performed for us? Think about it, Ezra – the Exodus, the Ten Commandments, the Torah, the rebirth of our state, to mention just a few. Isn't that enough?'

'There is much in what you have said, Simon. But one should not forget the Inquisition, the pogroms, the Holocaust – the murder of millions of innocent men and women, including one and a half million little children.'

'Please, Ezra, let me explain, and you'll soon realise what you – like many other naive people – have overlooked. I once heard a wise and eminent rabbi expound upon the meaning of the Holocaust. He asked us to imagine a simpleton, who had never seen a dentist in his life, sitting in the waiting-room. On hearing a scream from the surgery, he runs towards the door and presses his eye to the keyhole. And what does he see? In a complicated chair, among many strange instruments, lies the helpless screaming victim, and over him, wielding a pair of gleaming pliers dripping with blood, stands the merciless, white-coated torturer. Do you think (the learned rabbi asked us) that this man peering through a keyhole can behold the entire picture? Can a man like this possibly understand that, behind the closed door, the dentist – who the simpleton thinks is a common murderer – is performing a merciful act of healing?'

'Forgive me, Simon. How silly of me not to remember that the King of Kings holds a degree in dentistry.'

AN ASPIRING STORYTELLER

Just after Albert's twenty-third birthday, which coincided with his graduation from the faculty of medicine, his father invited him to his office. 'I have heard that you did very well in your final exams. Needless to say, son, I am very proud of you. But now it's time to think of your future. Are you perhaps considering specialising, or do you intend eventually to join an existing general practice?'

'No, dad,' the boy replied. 'I do not intend to become doctor. I'm going to be a storyteller.'

'My God, after everything you've achieved, you still. . .'

'Dad, we've been through all this before. You made me study medicine, but my heart has always been in writing.'

His father sighed deeply and leaned back in his chair. 'Fine,' he said, 'you're twenty-three. You have the right to live your own life. I've seen some of your writing – amusing little pieces. But tell me, what sort of stories do you intend to write now, for a living? More bedtime stories to lull people to sleep?'

'No, dad. My stories will be *wake-up* stories.'

'Wake-up stories? Wake-up to what?'

'To life.'

The father pondered this. 'And tell me,' he resumed at last, 'have you already picked a writer whom you would like to emulate? Perhaps a Chekhov, a Cervantes; or maybe a Gogol. . .'

'Dad, that would be too tall an order.'

'I see.' For the first time, his father smiled. 'Permit me, son, to tell you a little story *I* once heard, when I was still a youth. It may even be of some guidance to you, as you pursue your literary ambitions.' He leaned forward. 'Back in Poland, where as you know I came from, there were many impoverished writers – devoted storytellers. On long winter nights, huddled with their disciples (and yes, I was one of them) around a warm stove, they spoke in a sweet Yiddish and with innocuous envy about the great masters they hoped one day to become.

'Amongst us was this pale, haggard young boy with burning eyes, a poet, who one evening quite innocently asked our master: "Why should one aspire to be as great as Tolstoy, or Goethe, or the greatest of them all, Shakespeare?"

'Our master answered at once, with quiet modesty and without a hint of reproach. "You see, young man," he said, "if I didn't aspire to be like one of *them*, I would not even be what I am now."'

LUNCH WITH ANDREW

My neighbour Andrew, grey-headed, always dressed in a three-piece navy-blue suit with a white shirt and red tie, was a quiet man. His tiny wife Gretel walked like a shadow at his side, twining her frozen fingers into his soft warm hands. They had arrived in Australia from Hungary just before the war, and soon afterwards took up residence in our street, moving into a white two-storey house fronted by a heavy non-negotiable mahogany door. Since no one in the street seemed to know the couple's name, we referred to them as the Millionaires.

One rainy day, as I was waiting for a tram after work, a dark-blue Holden sedan pulled up abruptly at the kerbside, showering me with a mist of rainwater. The driver leant across and wound down the passenger window. 'Like a lift?' asked the smiling Millionaire. That was how we became friends. Since his office was not far from my place of employment, we agreed to have lunch every Wednesday in a nearby café.

I made a point of paying for our first meal together, and from then on we would take turns picking up the tab. What quickly became apparent, however, was that on Andrew's Wednesdays we ate a skimpy toasted cheese-and-tomato sandwich washed down with a Coke, while on *my* Wednesdays the fare was a fine chicken schnitzel, embroidered with corn or sweet cabbage, and finished off with a decent piece of strudel and a steaming cup of filtered coffee.

Well, I told myself, if one wants to keep up with millionaires, one has to pay.

There came a particular Wednesday – let's call it Sad Wednesday – when Andrew, stooped and red-eyed, staggered into the café. He seemed a broken man. 'Andrew,' I cried before he had even sat down, 'what's the matter?'

'You wouldn't believe it,' he replied, trying to compose himself as he slumped into his usual seat opposite me. 'Last Thursday, in the middle of the night, my Gretel took ill and had to be rushed to hospital. The doctors have already told me to prepare myself for the worst.'

'Andrew, but that's terrible. I'm so sorry. . .'

'That's not all. A few days ago I remembered that I haven't bought a plot for Gretel at the cemetery.' He was about to continue but just then our meal arrived. Andrew seemed to welcome the distraction and attacked his schnitzel (this being one of *my* Wednesdays) with surprising gusto. I knew he wanted to talk, but I was content to let him set the pace. It was not until he had swallowed his last morsel of strudel that he seemed ready to resume the conversation. He took a sip of coffee and immediately lapsed into his earlier air of despondency.

'Perhaps you can advise me in all this,' he said. 'Yesterday I contacted the cemetery people, about a plot for my Gretel. I really should have thought about it long ago – don't ask how much they're demanding these days for a measly piece of earth. You could just about erect a double-storey factory for that amount! Anyway, they made me an offer. If I buy a double plot, they drop the price. What a *chutzpah*! So I asked the black-coated huckster what they would do with my half if I happened to be, say, in America when I died. "We'll bring you back," he replied without skipping a beat.'

'That doesn't seem so unreasonable,' I offered cautiously.

'Give me a break! They'll bring me back, all right – at *my* expense. You know how I hate ships; and flying costs a fortune!'

RESURRECTING EVIL

Xavier François Lobel, thirty-year-old nobleman, colonel in the Foreign Legion stationed in the vicinity of Casablanca, was a man of contradictions. Gregarious, yet devoted to solitary desert walks; at daybreak imbued with a restless curiosity, at sunset haunted by melancholy.

One morning in the spring of 1859, Xavier left his barracks at dawn without saying goodbye to his adjutant. Being a man with an unquenchable thirst for knowledge, he understood the language of the desert, its animals and birds, and was captivated by its infinite beauty and vastness. He was intrigued especially by its silences, and the deceptive calm that guarded the treachery of its golden sands.

When Xavier set out, the air was quite crisp; but as he pene-trated deeper into the desert, the sun usurped the zenith and a vertical barrage of scorching rays assailed his head without mercy. He spotted some meagre but inviting shrubbery nearby, and although he knew he should not risk falling asleep, he stretched himself out on his beloved sand to rest his tired bones for at least a minute or two.

Suddenly he heard the voices of two eagles circling above. 'Father, I'll swoop down on him,' the smaller one was saying, 'and within no time I'll pick out his eyes.'

'No, son, don't do that,' the other replied. 'The man may not be asleep. He could be lying in wait for you.'

But how many sons will listen to a father's advice? For indeed, no sooner had the young eagle alighted upon Xavier than he found himself imprisoned in the colonel's powerful hands.

The father eagle was distraught. 'Please, sir,' he pleaded, 'set my son free. He is only a callow youngster. Look – I have a magical blade of grass. It can restore life to any dead creature. Take it, take it, in exchange for my son's freedom.'

Xavier frowned. He doubted that such a thing could be possible, but his insatiable curiosity had been aroused. He agreed and the deal was done.

On the way back to his camp, however, Xavier felt a profound unease about the whole affair. He wasn't sorry for letting the eaglet go; but how could he, an experienced officer, have been so incredibly gullible? The old eagle was obviously nothing but a crafty desert cheat, and he, Lobel, had managed to fall for its trickery.

As he was walking and reflecting thus, he came upon a huge dead dog lying across his path. It had an evil countenance, its eyes glassy but still enraged, and there were three bullet-holes in its head. 'What can I lose?' he thought. He placed the blade of grass against the beast's nose.

The massive dog sprang. Within moments, the noble Xavier François Lobel was no more. Licking its chops, the animal trotted off towards the camp.

THE SPECIALIST

At the earliest transcendent hour, while the first breath of light was still enmeshed in the dark bosom of sleep, an execution took place in a fortress built by Peter the Great. As a result of a failed attempt on the life of the cruel police commissioner Andrei Sergeyevich Sokolnin, who took great delight in torturing his victims, seven revolutionaries were hanged. Among them was the twenty-year-old Ivan, brother to Alexei Mikhailovich Lupov, a member of the assassination arm of Narodnaya Vola (People's Will) – an organisation which had adopted murder as the only instrument to combat the atrocities committed by the government against all political prisoners.

At the very next meeting of the assassination arm, Alexei Mikhailovich – known as 'The Specialist' because he never failed – volunteered to banish the despicable Sokolnin from the face of the earth. A few weeks later, at the hour chosen for the ambush, Alexei lay in a ditch, waiting for the coach that was carrying the marked man. Against his chest he cradled the home-made bomb that would execute the assassin's terrible will.

Alexei had calculated precisely the time when the coach would pass the spot selected as his enemy's rendezvous with death. He felt great joy and pride that he had been granted the privilege of dispatching this creature to the very gates of Hades. He had no doubt of his mission's success. It was not for nothing that they called him The Specialist.

He checked his watch. His guest was slightly late, and he wondered what could have detained a man renowned for his punctuality. Could it be that some vague premonition had caused him to alter the routine he so meticulously observed? But although Alexei did not let such thoughts unsettle him, every second that elapsed sharpened his nerves, each minute seemed an eternity.

Suddenly a signal from his team in the adjacent forest – all was in readiness, the coach was on its way. Yet at that moment Alexei sensed that something was not quite right. He couldn't locate the cause of his unease. He waited; the tension became unbearable. But he was The Specialist, and he would not fail.

The clatter of hooves deadened all other thoughts. Adrenaline flowed through his body like an electric current. He withdrew the bomb from beneath his loose overcoat, placed a hot kiss on its cold face. 'God speed,' he told it.

For the briefest of instants, as Alexei raised up his body to hurl the deadly projectile, terrorist and victim glimpsed each other's face. Andrei Sergeyevich shouted something. The coachman, noticing the black object in Alexei's hand, whipped at his horses furiously and accelerated with a great din past the crouching figure, leaving behind only a swirling cloud of dust.

Late that night, by the flicker of a dripping candle, Alexei Mikhailovich sat in the midst of his assembled comrades. He had not yet spoken, and a profound bitterness burned in his heart. At last the only woman present, Vera Figner – the same Vera Figner who had taken part in the assassination of Tsar Alexander II – asked the question on everyone's lips. 'Why, Alexei? What happened? What stopped you from finishing the job?'

The Specialist lifted his eyes. 'Little Nadezhda Andreyevna,' he replied slowly. 'She was sitting in her father's lap.'

THE JUDGMENT

It is difficult to describe the festivities in heaven in honour of Maurice the Jewish poet's arrival on a cloud of crematorium smoke. An angel ushered him into the paradise dining-room, where to his amazement a roasted duck, with a fork and knife in its beak, flew in and gently placed its outstretched neck before the famished poet. 'Please, sir,' it whispered, 'I'm kosher.'

Afterwards, two female angels carried him over to the paradise library. Maurice had never seen such a wealth of books, or so many unfinished manuscripts by short-lived writers. When he glimpsed the exquisite gold-encased Bible glinting from across the room, the holy book, of its own volition, floated down from its privileged uppermost shelf and settled on a lectern before him. As if to help him read, a warm breeze began to fan its pages. But no sooner had the pages ceased their riffling and paused at the Song of Songs, than the adversary – dressed in a black cape, his face painted white – entered through a keyhole.

'Aha!' said Satan. 'Caught you, you old voyeur!'

'Pardon me, your grace,' chimed a half-naked female angel who had been cataloguing some books in a corner. 'Everyone here is innocent until proven guilty.'

The hearing was scheduled for the evening. As he was ushered into the paradise courtroom, Maurice noticed the adversary whisper something to a technician, who at once switched on a cloud-shrouded moon. Behind a long bench covered with green felt sat a lame-looking public official. 'Poet,' an angelic voice murmured into Maurice's ear, 'you're in trouble. This judge is an ignoramus. He is the very one who sent Kohelet to Hell – and just for those three little words, *All is vanity*.'

Maurice was bewildered. This situation was entirely incongruous with his earlier reception. But he had no time to think, for the adversary, who had taken the witness stand, was jabbing towards him with a surrealistically elongated finger.

'Your honour,' the adversary began, in a shrill falsetto, 'this man belongs to me!'

A trio of merciful angels stood up in the gallery. 'But he just arrived from the worst concentration camp on earth,' they chanted in unison.

'And so he did,' the black one conceded. 'But listen to the seditious lines this so-called poet penned during his journey to us.' He cleared his throat theatrically to recite the evidence.

'Heaven
Land without windows or a door,
What a roomy place you are,
Your god a dead metaphor.'

The judge rose unsteadily from his gilded fauteuil, his face dark as a funeral on a rainy day. Lifting his hand heavenward, he declared:

'Take him away, noble Satan. He's yours.'

THE ART OF EXILE

Bruno Schultz, renowned poet and painter, was born in 1892 in the Galician border town of Drohobycz, which now belongs to the Ukraine. Schultz was Jewish, but he felt little or no affinity with the Jews. And even though Hebraic folklore wove an ancestral thread through the fabric of his imagination, he considered himself – intellectually, spiritually and historically – a Pole through and through. Perhaps, as in many such cases, he had forgotten to consult with his neighbours, who would readily have informed him what he really was.

From the photograph of Schultz that appears in the *Encyclopaedia Judaica*, and even more so from his art, his poetry and his prose, including a translation of *The Trial* by Kafka, one can surmise that he did not create for pleasure or fame, but only for the common good. And like Kafka, whom he resembled both spiritually and physically (the same triangular face, the same deep brown eyes, even the same sartorial style), he too gave his life to the trade he loved, which made him – like most authentic artists – no man's master and no man's slave.

In 1942, when Germany invaded Drohobycz, the great dreamer suddenly became aware that he had evolved into the very protagonist of his own metamorphoses – those reveries in which he so masterfully fused the magical with the absurd. He, the Pole, had become the hunted Jew with nowhere to run.

As soon as Fritz Landau – a Gestapo agent, and one of those appointed to keep 'order' in the town – sniffed out Bruno Schultz and his provenance, he 'invited' the artist to adorn the wall of his little son's room with pictures from the stories of the Brothers Grimm. It was an invitation Schultz could decline at his peril. One evening, as the east wind that had howled all day abruptly subsided and a fluffy white snow began to drizzle, Bruno, the captive who was yet a free spirit, stepped out to buy a loaf of bread. How could he have known that lying in wait for him in a dimly-lit corner of the street was the Gestapo agent Günther, who harboured a grudge against Landau. Without a word, Günther opened fire at point-blank range. And so it was that this famous but tormented artist who had lived life as a Pole finally died as a Jew.

And it also happened that those painted walls, on which Schultz had immortalised a few fairy-tales for an innocent little boy, found their way mysteriously into the museum at Yad Vashem. They subsequently became an object of international contention, with Poland, Ukraine and Jerusalem all claiming ownership – ownership of some wall-paintings created by a solitary artist who had wanted so much to belong, yet did not belong to anyone, and ultimately not even to himself.

JUSTICE

Alfred Dreyfus, a Jewish captain in the French army, was falsely accused of treason. In 1894, at the age of thirty-five, he was brought to trial, court-martialled, stripped publicly of his rank and transported to Devil's Island. But as the story goes, there appeared a man named Émile Zola, who bravely stood up against this travesty of justice and proved the whole affair a sham. Eventually the verdict was reversed and Captain Dreyfus was exonerated.

In 1942, seven years after his death, in the depths of France's spiritual winter, Alfred Dreyfus was back on trial. And once again his country was a divided landscape, but it was a landscape without Zolas. The adversary was in the ascendant, and held sway over a minuscule, anaemic, stuttering minority.

Captain Dreyfus, in shrouds, is brought into the court. The prosecutor, a coiled spring, takes the floor. He cannot contain his excitement – it's payback time at last. He whips a white perfumed handkerchief from his pocket, wipes at the beads of sweat pearling his brow.

'Alfred Dreyfus,' he thunders. 'You are guilty of a heinous crime against the glorious French army, a crime for which you must, once and for ever, die!'

'But sir,' the prisoner replies. 'I was proven innocent.'

'That is exactly what you are guilty of.'

THE WINNING LOSER

> He played a game of chess with God
> And he bet the morning sun;
> In dream he beat Him once or twice,
> Though he never left square one.

He was born in the lap of a pale moon's chant, a pang in his heart and a smile on his lips. One day, while still a youth, he was assailed by a gentle yet awesome longing, a hankering he could not name. It spoke to him of mankind's universal pain, of humanity's waxen Icarus wings, of the fate of Sisyphus, and of his own incomprehensible lot. He began to cry like a child.

Suddenly he heard a voice, the voice of a goddess, or of a Muse. 'Yes, my poor child,' said the voice, 'you must indeed weep – more and more, so that posterity might sing. Look, I am gathering up all your tears. I shall fashion them into a string of exquisite pearls to adorn the neck of the German people. Surely they will bestow their warm thanks upon you, and ensconce you forever in the pantheon of their literary giants.'

Some hundred and thirty years later he revisited his beloved Berlin, where he had once hoped to be appointed to the professorial chair of German literature. He was stopped by a guard with the face of an obese clown. 'Why have you come here?' the guard asked gruffly.

'To discover how it goes with our beautiful Lorelei,' the visitor replied.

The guard's fleshy face broke into a grin. '*Ach, mein lieber Gott, sie is doch wunderbar.*'

'And what of Heine, the poet?'

'Never heard of him,' said the guard.

FUGUE OF DEATH

Paradoxically, Paul Celan, the German-speaking Romanian poet who called himself an Ashkenazi Jew, died of the song he lived for. Singing to his almighty *No-One*, he faithfully proclaimed that all poets are Jews. Having emerged out of the European Mitzraim, towards a new life under blue skies, albeit overgrown forever with black forget-me-nots, Celan never stopped singing.

There are stories based on legends, stories that unequivocally belong to the shadowy valleys of doubt; there are other stories which, though equally aglow with the mystery of legend, nevertheless blossom on the buoyant daylight slopes of believability.

On 20 April 1970, on a spring day during Passover in Paris, after a long walk through a forest of leafless weeping willows presided over by a wingless brown owl, Celan returned to his empty apartment on Avenue Émile Zola, just across the quay from the Pont Mirabeau. It was the first Seder night. Sitting alone at the head of a bare table, he began to chant, in the voice of his murdered father, his own strange *Haggadah*:

And You, O great No-One: You heard our moaning, You saw our tears, You witnessed the slaughter of millions of little children. All of this must have moved You. And so, not through an angel, not through a seraph, not through a messenger, but You, holiest No-One of all No-Ones, You Yourself came down from Your golden throne and, with an outstretched arm, led Your chosen out of the hell of affliction.

Then, in order not to break the ancient Passover custom, Celan drank the traditional four goblets. Goblets of his own black milk. And so, happy and tipsy and singing his Death Fugue to freedom, he sauntered towards the bridge that crossed the Seine.

Suddenly he heard the clatter of hooves, the crash of chariots, the barking of dogs, the scream of German-speaking Egyptians; and around him he saw a crowd of frightened camp Jews. 'Jump, brethren, jump!' he shouted. 'On the opposite bank lies our promised land. Our *No-One* will part the waters. Have faith – we have nothing to lose, and everything to gain!'

But they wouldn't move. Perhaps they couldn't. Only he, like the biblical Nachshon ben Aminadav, responded to the call. Celan straightened, stepped forward, and plunged into the swirling, sunset-reddened river.

DIALOGUE WITH A DESK CALENDAR

It was dusk on the last day of December. The year had almost reached its exit. As I began to unscrew the metal clasp that had held together the past twelve months, I heard a rustling whisper. It seemed that my desk calendar was addressing me.

'Sir,' it said, 'can you foretell the future of one's used-up days?'

I knew well the meaning of this painful question, but instead of answering *There is no avoiding the inevitable*, I found myself declaring: 'Days stream by like murky rivers into the eternal sea of time, which never overflows.'

'Nice words, sir,' said the calendar. 'Almost biblical. It's easy for you to philosophise, while we pages are eyeing the rubbish bin of oblivion – an oblivion we're about to be consigned to. What consolation can there be, in the loss of one's tongue, one's memories, one's psyche, one's very soul?'

'That's not so,' I retorted, intent on being conciliatory. 'Your life is not being ended – rather, *transcended*, assuming a distinct new form.' I was arguing like a cleric.

'*Ex*-tinct new form, more like it,' whispered the dying 31st of December. 'Please, sir, our fate lies in a simple question – a question that you, perhaps for reasons of delicacy or tact, refuse to answer. But we must call a spade a spade; this is not the time for iridescent illusions. We know that each of us owes our life to death, and there are no miracles, no mirages. That is the ultimate reality.'

I fell silent. I would never have believed that a calendar of days gone by could have sounded so utterly disenchanted.

THE KABBALIST

Winter of 1941 in the ghetto. Amid papered walls glittering with frost, at a table lavishly empty of food, beside the mocking smile of a dying stove, sat Reb Zelik and his ten-year-old son.

'You see, my son,' Zelik was saying, 'after the war between Gog and Magog there will be no more days to count. All ends will come to an end, and the Earth will be laid waste. And when each surviving Jew believes that he is the only one left in the world, the prophet Elijah will emerge and proclaim the arrival of the son of David, the true and only Messiah. And the Messiah, astride a mighty white horse and dressed in the mantle of spring, will reignite the extinguished sun and reawaken God's earth from its slumber.'

'But Father, why can't the Messiah come right now?' asked the boy. 'Why does he have to wait until there are no more days, until all ends come to an end?'

His father nodded. 'There is a story told by a great biblical scholar – though I believe it existed even before the scholar was born.'

'How can that be, Father?'

'Well, every word in this story, and every letter, is actually a hidden angel. These angels dwelt in various of the nine heavens, but one day they all joined together, and out of their close joining arose this short but extraordinary tale. Listen: *Chained to the gates of Rome lies a leprous old beggar and waits. This is our Messiah.*'

The boy looked puzzled. 'Is that it? Is that all?'

'Yes, that's all. That's the whole tale.'

'What is the beggar waiting for?'

'He waits for us, son.'

'Then why don't we go to him?'

'We have forgotten how.'

'Can we not learn again?'

Zelik lifted up his sad eyes. 'Black night, white snow,' he replied. 'And the road across the deep river is paved with thin ice.'